STORIES FROM

free

Books by A. L. Rowse

Stories
Night at the Carn
Cornish Stories (out of print)
West-Country Stories (out of print)

Autobiography
A Cornish Childhood
A Cornishman at Oxford
A Cornishman Abroad
A Man of the Twenties

Cornwall
Tudor Cornwall
The Cornish in America
Sir Richard Grenville of the *Revenge*
Three Cornish Cats

Shakespeare
Shakespeare's Sonnets. *A Modern Version*
Shakespeare's Self-Portrait. *Passages Chosen*
The Poems of Shakespeare's Dark Lady
Prefaces to Shakespeare's Plays

Elizabethan
The Elizabethan Age. 4 vols
Eminent Elizabethans
Christopher Marlowe: A Biography
The Elizabethans and America

Poetry
A Life: Collected Poems

STORIES FROM TRENARREN

A. L. Rowse

WILLIAM KIMBER · LONDON

First published in 1986 by
WILLIAM KIMBER & CO. LTD
100 Jermyn Street, London SW1Y 6EE

© A. L. Rowse, 1986
ISBN 0−7183−0590−6

Typeset by Scarborough Typesetting Services
and printed and bound in Great Britain by
Biddles Limited, Guildford and King's Lynn

To
Andrew Wilson
admirable novelist, scholar, friend

Contents

	Preface	9
I	How Dick Stephens Fought the Bear	11
II	The Influence of the Planets	17
III	The Lady Macbeth of Trewardreva	22
IV	Miss Pengrugla and Mr Roseudgeon	27
V	Who was Miss Flavell?	39
VI	Hotel Bedroom in War Time	43
VII	Polly of Trethurgy	51
VIII	The Fan	57
IX	The Rocking Horse	65
X	Blue Waves	73
XI	The Will	82
XII	The Doctor's Family	87
XIII	The Collaborator	93
XIV	The End of the Trewinnards	105
XV	The House at the Cross-Roads	108
XVI	The Bishop	118
XVII	The Inheritor	124
XVIII	The Amateur Archaeologist	130
XIX	How our College came to be Founded	137
XX	The Nibbled Bread	141
XXI	Psalm 109	145
XXII	Miss Tryphena and Miss Euphemia	150
XXIII	Captain Pollock's Fields	157
XXIV	Dereliction	159
XXV	The Ex-Schoolmistress	167
XXVI	Sandy Trebilcock's Farm	169

Preface

A local historian is bound to be much interested in folklore, and I find that, in going through this collection, it gives an authentic picture of the way Cornish life was in former days. I am not in the least interested in contemporary demotic society, or its characteristic stories of drinking and drugging, thugging and mugging — too boring and common, like the daily newspapers.

With Flannery O'Connor, about the best short-story writer of the century, I am interested only in the uncommon and odd, the queer things that happen in remote nooks and corners in the country — not the horrors and squalors of modern urban life *à la* Colin MacInnes and such writers. They are more in fashion, more pushed across by the media; but a historian doesn't care tuppence for fashions — he knows too well how they change. *They* will not like these stories — what matter? These are the kind of stories that I like — and others do too, I find. I am grateful to my publishers for encouraging me to collect them and urging me to write more.

Trenarren,   A.L.R.
St Austell

'How Dick Stephens Fought the Bear'
was first published in *West-Country Stories*,
Macmillan & Co Ltd, 1945.

I

How Dick Stephens
Fought the Bear

Have you never heard how Dick Stephens fought the bear? In its time people knew that story from Penzance to Plymouth, and the old men know it still. But alas, not the young ones. My father knew it, and held Dick in great account for it: as indeed he should, for Dick was a splendid fellow. Besides which he was a connection of our family. My father had told me before to get Dick one day to tell me the story. And last night at Trenarren I met him coming home from market, and he 'up and told' me, as we say. I write it down for the benefit of posterity; if I don't, the story will perish, when Dick and his generation die out, and the young people ought to know the prowess of their fathers.

But I wish I could give you some idea of the action, the vigour of gesture and speech of the old man. He had been very ill with bronchitis some four years ago and it had aged him. He was now in his seventy-fourth year he told me, after a little preliminary bantering, like a woman, about his age.

''Ow old shud 'ee think?'

'Sixty-two,' I said politely; and it was true, he looked a man still in his sixties.

'Se'mty-four nex' birthday,' he said and with an air of triumph.

'How long ago was it since you fought the bear?' I said, putting the leading question at once. He had never told me the story before, and somehow I thought this evening he might. There was nobody about: a beautiful July evening after rain – I had been watching the shades of colour on fold upon fold of the land going all the way up to Brown Willy and Rowtor, Kit Hill and the tors of Dartmoor on the sky-line; an unnaturally prolonged amphitheatre of coast-line, so clear was the evening, running all the way from Chapel Point beyond Mevagissey to the Gribben in the foreground, then to Rame Head and beyond Plymouth to Start Point – a good fifty miles – a world of coves, shingle beaches, dappled cliffs, and deep evening-blue water.

There in the lane was Dick, the farmer of Trevissick, before me, his arms shrunken, neck shrivelled, and a good bit bent; but still standing over six feet in his socks and his eye bright though a little sunken. The bell at Penrice sounded mellow and clear out over the rook-laden woods and the deer-park. I thought he might be willing to tell me, but I had no idea what a performance it would be – one in a thousand. To make sure, I told him father had always told me to get him to tell me the story, but had never told me himself.

'Well, – it must 'a been fifty-one or fifty-two year ago. I was a young chap, twenty-two, I remember – I mind as if it was yesterday. 'Twas one evenin' after work, and I walked into town in nothin' but me shirt-sleeves and old clothes – I thought nothin' of walkin' in to town. There was a fair down to Fair Park, an' crowds of people. An' there was a wrastlin' saloon with a notice op an' two chaps – Guest they was called, from South Wales: "'Oo would wrastle the bear?" 'Ee was proper trained for it you knaw. They 'ad a leather aapern, a g'eat blacksmith's aapern for 'ee to put on to protect 'ee from the bear's claws: rolled up 'ee was. An' 'twas, "'Oo wud fight the bear? "Oo wud wrastle the bear?" Nobody wud come forward. I went down with y'r uncle Bill – reglar sportin' man 'ee was: anythin' for a bit o' sport. An' 'ee said, "Damn 'ee Dick, go in and fight the bugger" – that was 'ow 'ee used to talk. Well – I was a bit bashful and never one for pushin' meself forward. An' when they said "'Oo'll fight the bear?" your uncle said "'Ere, mister, I've got a man that'll wrastle your bear." So after that I 'ad to, like. So I said to'n, "Darn 'ee, then, I will." An' 'ee op an' eaved out the aapern – 'ee was all rolled up – out over th'eads of the crowd. When they 'eard that somebody was goin' to wrastle the bear, they come in in 'underds.

'You knaw what a boxin saloon is like. Well – 'twas like that. But aw – I forgot – before I took on there was a chap called Bob

Saunders — live in town now, 'ee was a maason's labourer or else a maason, g'eat bi fellow 'ee was — aw fine fellow, g'eat arms on'n: '*ee* was goin' to fight the bear first. So we went in, and all the people come pushin' in — the plaace was crammed: I never saw nothin' like et. An' they 'ad a few rouns of boxin' and wrastlin', you knaw, like they do; and then Bob Saunders' turn come.

"Ee was the sort of chap that drink a lot, went round to pubs and anybody that was drunk 'ee'd op and giv'n a blaw an' knock'n out. That was the sort of chap 'ee was. Mind you a fine-built fella — aw — g'eat arms on'n. Well — 'ee took his plaace in one corner and the bear in th' other. Great brown bear 'ee was, four 'undered poun' weight. When they said "Time", 'ee rawse up from 'is corner on 'is 'ind legs and come forward — 'ee was trained to et. My God, Bob Saunders didn' stop to meet'n 'alf way: 'ee no sooner seed'n rise op on 'is 'ind legs th'n 'ee give one lep and lepped right over the rope in among the people.

'You should 'ave seed the people laugh. Laugh? Bob Saunders never 'eard th'end of it for months and months. People'd ask'n, "'Ow did 'ee fight the bear then, Bob? Deffer'nt thing to knockin' out drunk men in pubs, wudn' it?"

'Well, that put the wind up me a bit, I can tell 'ee. But I didn' say nothin'. They 'ad a few more roun's of boxin', you knaw like they do, and then my turn come. They put up the leather aapern on me, an' then before we begin, the man said, "There's two things I want for 'ee to understand, young man. This 'ere bear is muzzled. If you touch the muzzle 'ee'll bite your 'ead off. And the second thing is, you take'n on at your own risk; we wun't be responsible fur anythin' that 'appens."

'Well — they said that to put 'ee off a bit. 'N I was a braave bit frightened, but I didn' say nothin'. Well, they said "Time", and the bear got op from his corner, roase op on 'is 'ind legs and come forward. Mind you, I thought 'underds o' things. 'Ee come for to meet me and put out his g'eat arms an' we met. An' 'ee 'oogged me and I 'oogged 'ee. I cudn' shif'n. I tried to lift'n off his feet. But 'twas impossible. He was that weight, four 'underd pound. 'Ee was that firm—'

'Firm as a rock,' I put in.

'Ess, as a rock,' he repeated with emphasis and a sense of rightness. 'I tried'n this way, and I tried'n that way, and I cudn' move'n. I tried to give'n a cant, an' tilt'n over. I kicked at his leg, but 'ee wudn' let go. What was I to do with'n? I thought an' I thought: I 'ad 'old ov'm an' I didn' let'n go. An' 'ee was clever, trained to et. I noticed that 'ee was always trying to keep me op nuzzlin' under me chin and pushin' me op. An' once 'ee got one of 'is g'eat long arms right over me shoulder, and th'other under th'other. I thought me back was goin' to crack. But 'ee didn'.

'Then I thought that's 'is game, to keep me op. After that I kep'n down there, like that. I noticed 'ee was doin' all 'is work with his forearms; an' I thought if I can get 'old of 'is arms an' pinch they, 'ee wun't be able to do so much. So I got a 'old of 'is arms, an' I pinched 'em an' pinched 'em, an' I didn' let go. I was sweatin' like a bull, and I could feel 'ee pantin' an' strugglin'. An' I thought, Now, mister, I've got 'ee. An' sure 'nough I 'ad. I 'eld on and went on pinchin'n like this—'

Here it was necessary to give me a demonstration. Farmer Dick threw down his raincoat on the grass by the roadside under the bush of honeysuckle, threw down his fairings and his stick; I threw my walking-stick down and had my arms clinched together.

'Tha's 'ow I held'n. I cud feel 'is breath comin' an' goin'. When the people saw I 'ad'n, they was shoutin' out, "Give it to'n, Dick. You've got'n. 'Old on, ole man. You'll do'n." And then I 'eaved'n op sideways and give'n a twist, and thrawd'n right over on 'is back.

'You should 'ave 'eard the cheerin'. You knaw what tes like — some kick-op. They said you cud 'ear the cheerin' op town.

'The fellow that run the shaw — 'ee was a decent sort of chap, 'ee said, "Well, tha' the first time that I've been served that trick, young man. 'Underds of people 'ave tried to thraw'n, but nobody yet 'ave been aable to do et." Then 'ee said, "Would 'ee tackle'n again?"

'Well, now me blood was op, an' I felt confident like I cud thraw'n; 'n I said, "Ess, I'll tackle'n and thraw'n again."

'An' all the people cheered, an' said, "Good ole Dick, you'll

thraw'n. Try'n again." An' I did. There 'ee was back in 'is corner
pantin', an' I was sweatin' like wan thing.

'Well, w'en they said "Time", 'ee come for me. 'Ee was angry,
min' you: never been thraw'd like that before. 'Ee come at me,
and got 'is fore-paw roun' the back of me 'ead: 'ee give me a
blaw, drawd blood, made me smart, I can tell 'ee. I got the
mark, a little mark, there now.'

We stopped to inspect the place, which I must confess, after
half a century, in the fading light was indecipherable.

'But this time I knew 'ow to thraw'n, an' it didn' take me long.
But before I thraw'd'n, he op with 'is 'ind leg, and give me such
a blaw in the guts — my God, it made me feel sick, fit to spew,
for a minute. But I got 'is arms pinched and it didn' taake me
long this time, I give'd'n a cant and 'eave'n right over, a'most
out into where the people was.

'You shud 'ave 'eard the cheerin'. Aw, my dear life, there was
some kick-op. I can mind it now, and all the people comin' op
town was tellin' 'bout it, 'ow Dick Stephens thraw'd the bear. I
didn' knaw et at the time, but et seems between the first an'
secon' roun' father was in town, and people said to'n, "Your boy
is down there goin' to wrastle the bear," and 'ee come in and saw
the second roun'. I didn' knaw then. But afterwards—

'Aw, I forgot to tell 'ee. I 'ad me shirt-sleeves op; and w'en we
was swayin' to and fro, the bear got 'is nawse op and through his
muzzle with a twick, 'ee twicked me sleeve right off be the 'em.
So in th' interval, 'ee falled down on me 'an', an' I put'n in me
pocket.

'W'en I got 'ome that 'evenin', mother was in the kitchen — I
can mind et as if 'twas yesterday; good mother she was to me an'
a mother to everybody — I come in an' I sit down in the chair.
An' I said, "'Ere, mother, 'ere's me sleeve for 'ee to mend."

'She said, "All right boy. Ow did 'ee come to tear'n like that?"

'So I said, "'Aw, I've been in town fightin' the bear."

'With that father come in and 'ee op and told the story. An'
all she said was, "You ought to 'ave a box on the side of your
ear." Wonderful mother she was to we. An' tha's about all was
said about it.'

The story had come to an end. It had been told with a wealth of action: the old man had put himself into it for me: he was re-living the experience that was the high-water mark of his life. His fine dark eyes flashed; strength came back into the shrunken arms. Once we had to scuttle into the hedge for a passing car; still the story went on. Now it was finished.

Farmer Dick has a splendid, broad-shouldered son, as strong as his father, in the Metropolitan Police. As a postscript, he added: 'W'en I was op to London with George an' we went to the Zoo, we saw a big brown bear. An' I said to'n, "There's a bear, George, like the one I fought in town that time." People d'knaw that story from Penzance to Plymouth.'

The sun was going down behind the woods of Penrice, as the sun was going down, gently, evenly, hardly perceptibly, for him. The mellow notes of the bell struck ten. It was time to part and go home our respective ways.

'Yes,' he said, 'it must 'ave been fifty-one or fifty-two year ago.' And a dark shadow, the shadow of time, came into his eyes.

II

The Influence of the Planets

Way out in the back of beyond on Bodmin Moor is a gorge, a deep cleft in the high moorland, with a farm up above it. The eastern side of that Moor is even less well known than Dartmoor, for no main road runs along or through that escarpment, merely rough tracks — and there are bogs.

However, high up above the gorge — with a view as if on top of the world — was a farm with the ancient name of Medros: which meant a cultivable patch in the middle of moor.

This was owned and worked by an unlikely couple. Or, rather, it was owned by the wife, a rather wizened wisp of a woman with gold-rimmed spectacles, several years older than her husband. He was a handsome big fellow, broad shoulders, broad in the beam, heavy as an ox and capable of lifting a hundredweight of potatoes with one powerful arm. He had married her for the farm. No children.

The little place was her inheritance, along with a vein of credulity that came from her Plymouth Brethren family and upbringing. Life with her man had worn most of her beliefs away — only the propensity to believe something remained. She thought she understood him — he was made on a simple enough scale, like an ox; but she didn't.

One day at chapel, where she still played the little organ when there was a service, the local preacher said teasingly:

'Can you keep him in order?'

'I try to,' she said brightly.

The fact was, she couldn't. She didn't know what he was up to outside work on the farm; rather house-bound herself, and oddly house-proud (wasn't the place hers, to do as she liked?), she knew little enough of his goings and comings.

However, unknown to him, she had her own inner resource —

whether consolation or compensation, her form of interest of mind or even intellectual pride: she had come to know about the Planets.

Up there, on that high roof of the world, like a local Pamirs, she had good reason to believe in their influence. Above was the high, over-arching sky in which those points of light, larger or smaller, revolved round with the wheeling globe.

She didn't know much about them, but could recognise Venus — which did little enough for her, and, to say truth, meant little to her. She knew the Pole Star, and the Dog Star, Sirius; perhaps Castor and Pollux — though hardly what they meant; and of course the Plough, and the Pleiades, the Milky Way.

Her knowledge gave her an inner sense of security, perhaps superiority — welcome enough in her solitary life. It had come about in an ordinary, familiar way.

The Moor was a haunt of the gipsies. One day there arrived at her door a handsome piece of a gipsy woman, dark as the remote race she came from, and as exotic: bright red scarves, gold-earrings, lustrous oiled black hair, coiled like the snakes on the Moor, and 'all the fires of Hell were in her eyes', as a local poet wrote.

She looked prosperous enough. Nor was it difficult to win the farm-woman's confidence — she wanted *something* to believe in.

And the gipsy began with a *coup* — sufficient to confirm any-one's faith, if one were given that way.

It all started with telling her fortune by cards. When the cards were spread out on the kitchen table, face downwards, the farmer's wife — let us call her Margery — turned up in succession an ace of spades and a seven of diamonds.

It is well known that the first is an exceptionally bad card — it means a Death in the family; the second, an exceptionally good one — it means Money.

Not long after, news came from the Upper Peninsula, the Cornish part of Michigan, running like Cornwall itself and shaped like it out into a sea (in this case the great Lake Superior), that an old aunt had died. She left to Margery a sum that amounted to a neat £1500.

Her faith was confirmed. It was only natural that the gipsy woman should claim her cut − of £50. It was the beginning of an acquaintance, rewarding on both sides.

For Margery now graduated to the Planets.

She had first to learn the astrological signs for them: the Sun ☉, Moon ☾, Mercury ☿, Venus ♀, Mars ♂, Jupiter ♃, Saturn ♄, Uranus ♅, Neptune ♆.

Well, wasn't that worth another £50 down?

It was arranged between them that she was to have a monthly lesson, at £50 each month on the gipsy woman's, Elvira's, round of the Moor.

Next month it was the signs of the Zodiac, the various 'houses' into which the firmament was divided − fascinating to observe the night-sky from on top of the world, not far from Hawk's Tor.

These had to be learnt in their relative order: 1 Aries, the Ram; 2 Taurus, the Bull; 3 Gemini, the Twins; 4 Cancer, the Crab; 5 Leo, the Lion; 6 Virgo, the Virgin; 7 Libra, the Balance; 8 Scorpio, the Scorpion; 9 Sagittarius, the Archer; 10 Capricorn, the Goat; 11 Aquarius, the Waterman; 12 Pisces, the Fishes.

These 'houses' were not remote from her experience − ram, bull, goat, fishes. Even the lion reminded her of an occasion in her childhood when Boswell's famous circus used to tour the country. Once a lion had escaped from its van, jumped a hedge into a field where an infuriated cow had chased it round, until it was forced to give her a pat in self-defence.

More difficult were the symbols that had to be learnt in their relative order, for the Zodiac is a circle in which each sign falls opposite to its proper 'house' or division, and it is necessary to know which sign is opposite to any given one.

This took another month, another £50 down.

Then came the general characteristics of the Planets when in the ascendant. Venus was obvious, and dominated love matters − not of much interest to her. Mercury was the Messenger, and had to do with messages, letters, news, money − of much more interest. Mars was equally intelligible: wars and rumours of wars (she remembered her Bible language here). The Moon, unexpectedly, was a watery planet, and therefore uncertain, unstable; in certain aspects it portended sickness, ill-health; in others, extravagance, gambling, waste.

More difficult were the conjunctions and appositions, favourable or unfavourable. These she applied herself to for a whole year, unable to master them for herself without the aid of her mentor with her charisma, her magnetic eyes.

What, for instance, to make of the conjunction of Venus and Moon: love conjoined with extravagance and waste? She could not make out the way in which Venus dominated her affairs — there was no love-interest in *her* life.

Perhaps Elvira knew a thing or two: she had a better idea than most of what went on around the Moor. Had she, so to say, stacked the cards — to change the metaphor, or perhaps called the cards in aid? Was she trying to tell Margery something?

For it must be said that Elvira believed her own science — her Magic, as she called it. People are much more effective with their Message, if they themselves believe it — as Hitler certainly believed his mania against the Jews, and put it across a notably credulous people.

All this went on for a full year, unbeknownst to Martin, out and about the fields; he had little interests of his own of which Margery was unaware. To all intents they lived separate lives — at any rate, in their essential interests, on different levels.

His special interest at this time was a caravan he was fixing up, ensconced in a tight little corner down in the gorge, out of sight of and as far as possible from the farm. Margery knew of its arrival, for she paid for it: a useful investment for summer visitors, it would pay for itself, he said.

There were incidental expenses for its equipment, a couple of beds, kitchen and cooking utensils, sanitary arrangements, etc. For which Margery paid. One way and another the legacy from her aged aunt in Michigan had come in very handy, but was rapidly diminishing.

The fact was that Martin was a full-blooded, passionate man, who could do with a great deal more sex than was available around the place, and wanted it regular too.

In a market town a dozen or so miles away he picked up a

young girl he fancied. Free and easy, and about eighteen, she was all too ready to meet his requirements. He was setting her up in the caravan. It was only too convenient, ready to hand, too fatally easy. The trouble was that, a passionate type, he was besotted on the biddable little creature, ready for anything, do anything he liked with her. Years older than she was, he did not think of consequences.

He did not consider that, for one thing, a mere chit of a girl might fancy a young fellow her own age, rather than this bull of a man who was a bit too much for her.

And what did the Planets tell Elvira about this complication?

She drew out the physical characteristics of Taurus, the Bull: 'squarely built, a bit stooping, short thick neck, full lips, hair dark and thick on chest and body.' Mental characteristics: 'obstinate, plodding, strong-willed, resentful, above all jealous.' In short, bull-headed. She scented danger.

She next consulted the cards, to define the area of danger. Without betraying her thoughts, she and Margery laid out the cards in regular form on the kitchen table. And drew out the dark man all right, the King of Clubs, in closest proximity to the Queen of Hearts.

On the second round of choice Margery drew the worst possible: the Ace of Spades — disaster, possibly fatal.

Shortly the Moor awoke to the news that a young couple had been found dead in a caravan in the gorge — shot dead, no one knew how, a gun beside them. Was it a suicide pact? Or had the young fellow shot the girl, and then himself? They were young to die. No one knew the explanation; it was a mystery.

But only for a week, or less. For, within the week, Martin's body was found on the Devon border, by the Tamar, where he had shot himself.

And thus the story could be pieced together — though Elvira disappeared from the scene for a time, until rounded up for obtaining money 'under false pretences'.

But were they false? Or, if so, to what extent?

III

The Lady Macbeth of Trewardreva
A Jacobean Tragedy

It was indeed made the subject of a 17th century play, George Lillo's *The Fatal Curiosity*, when the theatre was revived, after the too-long rule of the Saints, at the Restoration. The events it described had happened close to Penryn in Cornwall in the Jacobean age — actually in 1618, only a dozen years after the production of Shakespeare's *Macbeth* in London in 1606. Talk about 'nature imitating art' — here was a remarkable instance of life itself following a plot that might have been taken over, *ceteris paribus*, from the play.

These things happened in the family of a substantial yeoman farmer up at Trewardreva, above Penryn — the little port of the neighbourhood before Falmouth came into existence, also at the Restoration. I take it that Tre-war-dreva means the place-above-the water. It was then a good holding, pasture, meadow and a little wood, in the granitic, hard-faced parish of Mabe — as hard as the heart of Lady Macbeth herself.

Subsequently, after the fall of the family in circumstances I am about to relate, the property came into the hands of more prosperous proprietors, who had made money in shipping at Penryn. They proceeded to build the fine granite house around the end of that same 17th century, most of which has survived to us today, with richly decorated plaster ceiling in the great room upstairs.

Earlier in that century all was on a simpler scale — Cornwall had not yet emerged from the Elizabethan age, with its prolonged sea-conflict with Spain, piracy in the Channel, hand to hand conflicts on board the little coastal barks, private ventures into the Mediterranean and across the Atlantic to the Spanish Main.

A younger son of the farmer at Trewardreva was of a roving disposition, had no mind for a settled life on the land, and took to the sea. Here he had a happy semi-piratical career, and did well enough, until he met his come-uppance in the Aegean at the hands of the Turks. His little ship was overwhelmed, but somehow he managed to get on shore on the island of Rhodes. Sentenced to a term of imprisonment, he with a few of his comrades succeeded in escaping, and got back to London.

Altogether they were characteristic of the scores, if not hundreds, of venturesome sailors with their ups and downs in life, their comedies and tragedies, to be found along the wharves of Rotherhithe or Billingsgate, or whom we encounter in the pages of Simon Forman's Case-Books.

John Vosper's next venture was to take shipping for the East Indies, where again he did sufficiently well — in fact rather better, for he was able to sail for home with a belt full of gold pieces, the profits of his trading and speculation.

Taking ship for the West, he was cast on shore, but came a-land with his precious cargo of gold and jewels intact, safely stowed away about his person.

Making inquiry, he found that a sad change had come over his father's fortunes. Farming had failed with him, his farm contracted to a small-holding about the house, barely enough to keep body and soul together.

On his way up to the rocky, unwelcoming back-of-beyond, he called at his sister's wayside cottage. A grown man, bearded and be-ringed, barbaric gold rings in ears, unrecognisable for the boy who had gone to sea years before, he revealed himself to her, and imparted to her the good fortune he had brought back with him.

In return he learned from her that, after their mother's death, their father had re-married.

The sister had no good report to make of the woman.

The new lady at Trewardreva was in fact no lady. Very swarthy of complexion, raven-black hair greasily coiled like snakes upon her head, was she perhaps a gipsy? No one knew where she came from, except further up into the back-of-beyond, the moorland infested with adders.

She was an adder herself, stony-hearted as the rocks they lived among — though they not infrequently came out to sun themselves upon the boulders warmed in summer.

No warmth in her, nor did she make much of an appearance among the sparse neighbours about. Nothing neighbourly about her.

She had some excuse for her hardness. With a failing man for husband, much older than herself, practically all the work of their holding fell upon her — at any rate, all the heavy work. All he was fit for was feeding their few starveling cattle with such food as he could scrabble together — not much feed among those rocks and carns up there, all that was left to them after the fields and meadow, even the spinney, had gone.

They were miserably poor. With a heart embittered by poverty and resentment, she held her husband in contempt — she had hoped for better things earlier in taking him on — and in subjection. She could have killed him with a good will.

*

The daughter never visited the old home. But, with her brother's return and the hopeful new turn in their fortunes — for the sanguine young fellow, proud of his wealth, had revealed what he was carrying home — she would go up on the morrow to see how things were taken and would work out.

The brother went on his way and presented himself at the farm door as night came on. To no very favourable reception. His father had gone to bed. The son would not reveal himself, with his good news, until the morrow when his sister and he would together confront the old man with their good luck. A family reunion indeed, if not return of the prodigal son.

Meanwhile, he was refused what he badly needed, a night's lodging.

'No fly-by-nights 'ere', the woman said, holding the door half-open. A gold piece from his store persuaded her to open it and let him in. Within, she watched him out of the corner of her baleful eye, summing him and the situation up, while she laid him a scanty supper.

After what could scarcely be called a meal, he warmed

himself at the fire, and drowsy, but self-confident as ever, he boasted of his wealth, taking off the heavy belt that had weighed him down and dragged his steps.

He went off to bed, and slept soundly, never noticing the hungry look that lit up her eyes in the smoky gloom of the interior.

An hour or so later, sure that the unknown visitor was in the stupor of deep sleep, worn out by his journey, she stole up the stairs to her husband.

She awoke him with a hiss, rather than a whisper:

'Our chance be come.'

'What do 'ee mean?'

'Our one and only chance to saave ourselves.'

She explained to him the arrival of their chance visitor:

''Ee've a-gotten a pile o'money about'n.'

'What's that to us?'

'What's that to us, you fool: don't 'ee see?'

He felt her hot breath on his cheek:

'It's now or never; we'll never have a chance again. We must 'ave that money.'

''Ow?'

'Do'n in.'

Her husband was revolted by the idea.

'You lily-livered coward. What do 'ee taak me for? Do 'ee think I be afraid to do it meself?'

She showed him the big kitchen knife she had brought up with her.

'If you be afeared to do it, I be'n't.' Holding the knife to her trembling husband, she threatened to leave him, if he wouldn't strike a blow to relieve their poverty.

'Think I'm goin' on in this ole way for good an' all?'

She paused, while he hesitated.

'I'm goin' to do it,' she said, and arose from beside the bed and made for the door, knife in hand.

At that he got up to follow her lead. She propelled him through the door, across the passage, into the room where the unknown man slept his last sleep, and the deed was done.

*

Next morning the sister of the murdered man arrived, with the news of her sailor's return from sea.

There was a sinister silence in the house, the silence of the Seven Sleepers, or of death. It was broken by a feeble cry from the father, on the verge of fainting, and visible agitation on the face of his harridan of a wife.

Could it be the brother whom she had taken in the night before, and then broken irrevocably the sacred law of hospitality?

A simple test would tell. The farmer's son had always had a large scar on his chest, from having been gored by a bull as a boy.

Stricken by the horror of the night's doings, now further shaken by doubt, fear, suspicion as to what might be revealed, the old farmer pulled himself upstairs to the appalling scene in the bedroom, the blood-spattered bed. The light of day revealed the scar on the sailor's chest, and the truth that it was indeed his son.

With the same knife lying by, he cut his throat. The noise of his slump to the ground brought up his wife; who, grasping the meaning of the scene, followed suit.

The floor of the little rustic bedroom indeed resembled the last scene of a Jacobean tragedy, the stage littered with corpses of the actors in the act.

IV

Miss Pengrugla and Mr Roseudgeon

I had thought of calling this simply 'Miss Pengrugla'; however, it is by no means the whole of her story — if I knew it — but simply that aspect of it that concerned her relations with Mr Roseudgeon. Enough in itself — and more than enough for Mr Roseudgeon, an irritable man, who was much irritated by it.

The Pengruglas of Pengrugla — Cornish folk pronounced it Pengurgler — were good old yeoman stock, who had been on the place for many generations and were coming to an end with an only son and daughter. The name meant the end of a barrow, 'crug' in Cornish, and indeed that was the situation of the farm-place, a slight eminence was all that was left of the barrow from ploughing over the generations. Earlier, they sported even a coat-of-arms, if of questionable authenticity: three toads erect, sable.

Young Roseudgeon was of lower-class stock, but — very much an intellectual, and ambitious — was bent on raising himself into the class with which his tastes had most affinity — the old country gentry, whose hold on the land was failing. With his novels a success and now being filmed, he was making the grade financially; but he still had handicaps.

One of these was his first name, Eric: it represented the taste of his sister aged ten, when he was born. Girlish and ridiculous as he thought it, what was worse was that it bespoke an element in his nature which he did not wish to publicise. He *looked* masculine enough, but was not responsive to women, at any rate sexually. In fact he was a complex character, whom people could not quite make out.

Certainly not Miss Pengrugla, who was of a simple, forceful nature. She surely had personality and initiative; she knew how to run things, Women's Institutes, the local Conservative Party,

Church bazaars, all that sort of thing. She ran the large, neighbouring village from the farm she came to own. She was very public-spirited, and bent on cutting a public figure.

Eric — for all that his name was much more widely known — was not really public-spirited. The public — and Miss Pengrugla in particular — thought that they knew him. But they did not. As a writer, he lived in a world of his own. His inner life was all in all to him; he valued his privacy and would admit no one into it. This made him self-sufficient; he had a good conceit of himself, without appearing conceited.

Indeed, with his humble background, he gave the appearance of being diffident, needing help. The combination was provoking; and it provoked the superior Miss Pengrugla. She would make a man of him — and a career for herself.

With his polite, and apparently conformable, exterior it took her years to discover that he had a mind of his own. The more she pressed and tried to batter down his defences, the more resistance it built up in him.

She was a determined woman, but not a subtle one. He was a subtle, clever man. He came to dislike her, for all her evident, good qualities, always ready to help anybody. He did not need her help, though she thought he did. (Miss Pym diagnoses for us 'the universal concern of women for men.') Though not very practical, he had a feminine side to him, and more than feminine intuition. What she could never have understood was that, though they tangled, he was able to distance himself from his irritation, even vexation, and see the situation all round. It interested him as a writer, though as a man he was not amused.

*

Things began very well — promisingly from Miss Pengrugla's point of view. Her father was the steward — as the Cornish call the agent — of the estate on the hither side of Pengrugla. The young writer was ambitious to elevate himself in society by taking on the country house belonging to it, which was unoccupied by the ancient family of gentry to whom it belonged.

Pengrugla *père* was nothing loth to find a paying tenant, but his daughter was positively keen to have Roseudgeon there.

Preoccupied by his work, he did not tumble to the possibility that she saw herself as the lady of the manor — at least not for some time, until several indications pointed that way.

'Call me Dorothie, will you?'

He thought the spelling affected and silly, and firmly stuck to Miss Pengrugla, until he eventually capitulated to the form Dorothy, taking no notice of the would-be distinction.

For her part she shortened his name, rather coyly, to 'Mr Rose' — then to Rose. He thought this taking liberties, understandably touchy as he was about his name.

Not well educated, and not at all literary, she once ventured upon what she thought a joke — she had no sense of humour — and quoted, 'A rose smells as sweet under any other name.'

She had no idea where it came from, or that he hated clichés, literary pretensions from the not very literate.

Her one intellectual interest, if it could be called such, was old Cornish history and folklore. This gave her an excuse to borrow a book now and again from the large library he had now installed in the house big enough to hold it. At least nine or ten bedrooms, only four furnished as such — all the rest were bookrooms or studies occupied by books.

No family — just a housekeeper to look after him and his cat.

'The old country gentry have moved out, and the best-sellers have moved in,' he would say with some complacency. One or two more of his literary *confrères* who had settled in his native county came to mind.

He and Miss Pengrugla were at least natives; they had that in common, and their interest in local history made a bit of a bond. But it was a mistake to take advantage of her position, while her father was alive and in charge, to borrow the writer's books and hold on to them. Little did she realise how it irritated him, or how inconvenient for a writer — often wanting to look up something, and the book was not in its place on the shelves.

He was a fussy bachelor, and hated anything out of its place, particularly books he might want to consult at any moment.

'Isn't it far more important that they should be here?', he would fume to his housekeeper. 'What's the point of her reading anyway? What good does it do her? Her time is of no value, mine is,' etc, he would chitter angrily to his housekeeper.

'Tch, tch,' she would say peaceably. 'I'll ask her to return them.'

'That's not the point. I don't want them *out*. I want them *here*, and *now*.'

Impatient by nature, he had a point: a quotation to verify, a date to look up — and the particular book was not there when he needed it.

Eventually he put his foot down, and made it as clear as he dared to the daughter of the steward — who stood for his land-lord — that he did not like lending books.

People have no conscience about books, and a writer should never lend them.

*

When the steward died, the occupant felt a certain sense of release, that his occupancy was not contingent upon favour. He felt that much freer in his relations with Miss Pengrugla, who now had not even the exiguous lien she had before.

In the last weeks of the Second German War her brother was killed. Here was something of a bond of sympathy. She detested the Germans, and the writer hated their guts for ruining the age he lived in — initiating the reign of violence, mass-murder and terrorism that characterises the appalling 20th century. A good, unforgetting and unforgiving Celt, he recalled Tacitus' phrase for it — *furor teutonicus*. He regarded 1914 as the beginning of the end of civilisation.

Miss P. of course had never heard of Tacitus, but she knew how to organise sympathy.

Invited to lunch at a rather grand neighbouring house, he found that she was the only other guest. She was arrayed in deepest black, costume, silk scarf, gloves, even a hat at lunch: a formal expression of sorrow.

After lunch, would Mr Rose drive her home?

How had she come? Walked across the fields? — for she stowed away a pair of gum-boots in the boot of his car.

He drove her to her home, with no very good grace, for he was a poor driver. It involved going down an overgrown, twisting lane, granite hedges on either side where one could easily get stuck and impossible to pass anything. He called himself 'the world's worst reverser'.

Arrived at the rambling old house he encountered a pause, but it was only when he got home that his intuition told him the significance of it: she had deliberately *willed* leaving the boots in his car so that he would have to bring them back. He thereupon made up his mind that he would do nothing of the sort.

Inevitably a letter arrived: 'I am afraid that I left my gumboots in your car. Would you mind returning them when you are next this way?'

He was going away the following week; so he waited until the day before he left, and replied with a curt p.c.: 'I am off tomorrow for several weeks. Perhaps the next time you are this way you would collect them for yourself.'

In his absence they were collected.

*

He was not much of a party-goer, so that it was not easy to meet him, much less corral him. He had no intention of being, in the American phrase, 'roped and tied'.

However, a party was being given which he did attend. It was to celebrate the marriage of a young son and heir, happily returned from prison camp in Germany where he had spent the whole war, having been captured at Dunkirk.

Few were the people he knew. A lady quite unknown to him came up to say how much she enjoyed his books. To this ritual beginning he gave the ritual answer, and went on to ask politely where she lived. She gave the name of the house where Kilvert had visited in the Victorian age, where that inflammable heart had fallen in love with his hostess, and described it all in his Diaries.

The writer's interest was at once engaged. He might have followed it up and perhaps arranged an invitation to the house, when they got separated in the crowded room.

Incontinently came up Miss P., hot and flushed, with,

'My dear Rose, you can't possibly speak to that woman — she's a terrible woman.'

With that she flung off.

Roseudgeon had formally polite manners himself, if without real *politesse du coeur*, and was astonished at this outburst.

Who was the unknown lady? She might have been a murderess from this onslaught on her character, practically within earshot. Had she perhaps heard? She did not return to pursue the conversation, which might have led to something interesting.

How to account for it? Had Miss P. taken a drink too many? (Himself was a teetotaller.) She was evidently out of control with some feeling or other — was it jealousy, resentment that she had not been noticed?

What infuriated Roseudgeon was the proprietary attitude assumed. Miss P. had enjoyed a certain unspoken lien while her father was alive, with his authority over house and estate. But that was over — and 'Mr Rose' was nobody's fool. He fancied a career for himself.

The party was spoiled for him, and he left soon after. But he chalked it up as a bad mark against Miss P. and did not forget it.

*

It was a year or two later before she next had a chance of misconducting herself. Since he never invited her to his house, it was understandably at another party, which gave an opportunity of meeting him. This was at the home of the former MP for their constituency, a Tory as Miss P. was with conviction, and for whom she had worked with a will. She was a good organiser, with any amount of will — had her village under her thumb; there she was spoken of with respect and could organise anyone into anything.

Roseudgeon was politically on the Left, like most intellectuals at that time, and had fancied himself for that constituency. He took along to the party a fellow member of the intellectual Left who happened to be staying with him.

Once more an unknown lady made a bee-line for the writer she had read, but never met — a member of the County Council to the fore in good works. (Did Miss P. read? Apparently not — not even his books.) The large and lofty County Alderman rather monopolised him, and he was careful to steer clear of Miss P.

So that it was only on leaving that she pursued him and his friend to the door. Using his friend as a shield of defence, he pushed him into the breach. But it was at 'Mr Rose' that she directed her words. He was so anxious to escape that he didn't listen and couldn't make them out. She looked hot and flushed again.

Going away, Roseudgeon recommended her to his friend who was in need of a woman — himself was not. His friend was helplessly disorganised — couldn't run his life or his affairs. *She* would organise him — what he most stood in need of.

Roseudgeon was a little surprised that his friend did not welcome the idea at all, but put it aside at once.

Why not? Geoffrey was at sixes and sevens, was in dire need of pulling together. Miss P. was an expert hand at pulling things together. Geoffrey wouldn't even consider it: he preferred to stumble on, disorganised and helpless.

Then why did not Miss P. bring her guns to bear on the ex-MP for whom she had worked so devotedly? He was available, a bachelor, not averse to women, a house of his own for her to run — why on earth didn't she make for him?

The former MP — perhaps he wouldn't have lost his seat, if only he had married her — rather admired her appearance. She was very dark, with a mass of raven glossy hair, and a strong profile — she was certainly sharply etched. He considered that she had a marked Byzantine appearance. He shared her interest in Cornish folklore, and she thought herself descended from the Palaeologus who came to Cornwall in the Elizabethan age, lived on Tamarside as a country gentleman and had progeny.

In the church of Landulph there was his memorial, no doubt about it.

'Here lyeth the body of Theodoro Palaeologus of Pesaro in Italy, descended from the Imperyall Lyne of the last Christian Emperors of Greece: being the sonne of Camilio, the sonne of Prosper, the sonne of Theodoro, the sonne of John, the sonne of Thomas, second brother to Constantine Palaeologus, the

8th of that name and last of that lyne that raygned in Con-
stantinople, untill subdewed by the Tyrks. Who married with
Mary the daughter of William Balls of Hadleigh in Suffolke,
gent. and had issue 5 children, Theodoro, John, Ferdinando,
Maria, and Dorothy, and departed this life at Clyfton the 21st
of January, 1636–7.'

There was the name Dorothy, not Dorothie, by the way. Miss P.
might very well be descended from a Palaeologus, for all Roseudgeon cared. Her Byzantine appearance had no allure for
him, though he could see her dark and frowning in an ikon, or
the direct confrontation of her stare in an Empress in a man-
dorla. She was distinctly imperious, he never saw her smiling,
too intent on the end in view.

*

Her last attack came from the historical side. She had a nephew
on the female side – no Pengrugla – who was at one of the most
expensive of public schools, and was *very* interested in history
and literature. Might she bring him to tea?

It was a way of inviting herself to the house – some years after
he had come there, though he was much away in London, and
increasingly in America.

Was there anything more behind it? his suspicious mind
wondered. He had known a friend or two of his inclinations
marry a wife on account of the son she had by a previous
marriage, not for the lady herself.

Was this the bait – the youth to be sacrificed on the altar of
her will and intention?

Women *never* give up, he reflected. They were more per-
sistent than men – that was how many a weak-willed man was
coralled into marriage. She was a fool: she could perfectly well
have enjoyed a friendship with him over the years, but on his
terms, not hers.

She was used to having her own way, and must have supposed
all along that by pushing persistently enough the door would
eventually open to the blissful prospect: wife of a successful
writer, a celebrity, lady of the manor.

Her intended remembered a line of Montherlant, a similar disposition, impossible to corral, on the subject of marriage: '*Il avait nommé cette chimère "l'hippogriffe"*.' But Miss P. did not know French, nor had read the poem in which her Mr Rose had quoted it for epigraph.

However, here was a new approach – perhaps she had tumbled to the fact at last. He was curious to see the youth: she might bring him along.

He turned out a tall, rather good-looking young man, of robust, rustic appearance. He did not say much for himself at tea. Miss P. filled in for him with some trite historical remark – about the American War of Independence – as if something new, an enlightening discovery, when it was an elementary fact everyone learned at school. Mr Rose, always vexed by obtuseness, managed to convey this dampening thought. He could not abide elementary instruction from that quarter – or from any quarter. He was not an easy man to deal with.

Nor did the young man make a fist at history, or anything else. He was lucky to get a place at the university. There he spent much of his time, and all the money there was to see him through, on the race-course. Sent down by his college, and totally unqualified for anything, the stalwart young man found his level working on a farm.

What a fool, thought Roseudgeon, who had no feeling for horses and could hardly tell one end of a horse from another. And then added, 'What a family to be connected with!' Himself had no family to speak of, and no liking for family obligations.

Miss P. had a good heart, and did her best for her nephew. She set him up on a farm of his own. She informed Mr Rose of this new development, only when he inquired after the promising youth. Disappointed of her hopes in him, she was doubtful whether he would make a go of the farm. Mr Rose ventured to recommend marriage as the solution of his problem.

'What he needs is a good strong-minded wife to take control, and organise him properly,' said he sagely.

Miss Pengrugla agreed – 'if only he gets the right one,' she added, her confidence undermined.

*

Over the years they maintained passable, formal relations. Now and again she would ring him up to consult him as to some hobby of hers — restoring a Jubilee lamp-standard in the village, a coat-of-arms or hatchment in the church. He thought it usually nonsense, and disliked being badgered about such things.

In any case, like most writers, he loathed being telephoned. He never used the telephone except for business — he rang up no one, if he could help it.

One evening he received a surprise call for sympathy. She was leaving Pengrugla for her nephew to take over. She had never liked the farm or farming — 'such a chore, cows!' (What else did she think she was good for, reflected her listener: a literary career, correcting proofs, making an index? But he considered her doubtfully literate.)

'Oh, my valley! When I think of my valley — I can hardly bear to think of leaving it. I rang you up because I knew *you* would understand.'

She was on the verge of tears of self-pity.

He understood too well — self-induced tears. And, anyway, if she felt like that about her valley — last of her name to occupy it — why leave it?

He expressed some sympathy, without feeling it.

She was growing older. Perhaps she had at last given up on Roseudgeon. Not without a parting shot, however.

She came once again to the house, this time on the excuse of driving an eminent old princess, a recognised descendant of the Palaeologi who had taken to Cornwall. Roseudgeon, for his part, was much taken with the old lady as a literary and historical monument. She had known everybody, even the Imperial Court at St Petersburg — a civilised affair, compared with what succeeded it. With an apartment in Paris too, she was *au fait* with literary life there and had known Proust, was a close friend of the famous Abbé Mugnet.

Miss P. was out of all this; but she well knew the story of Roseudgeon's house, how he came by it, and also how he lived there. He was much away from it: it seemed the fate of that beautiful place to be deserted.

Flaring up at him, as usual, she got her own back on him by saying,

'You should live in the house properly.'

Here was her conclusion on the wasted years gone by. He knew too well what she meant: the house was meant for a family, he should have lived in it properly with a wife and family. Like everybody else.

But he was not like everybody else: he regarded conventional life, with wife and family, as the death of the spirit. He knew too that writers were — like Carlyle — 'gey ill to live with.' Himself had a satisfactory homosexual life — with his cat, a perfect companion for a writer. They doted on each other.

Then he too flared up, but within himself, as usual, under control.

'What business is it of hers how I live my life? Or how I live in this house? Or however much I am away? In fact, I would not be able to live in it but for America, universities, lectures, etc.'

He chittered away within himself.

Then he decided that at length he would show her, and where she got off. From that moment he steered the talk between himself and the old lady, kept it rigorously, snobbishly on the rails of their literary acquaintance, their grand friends — London, Paris, Washington, New York — and kept Miss P. completely out of it.

They all realised what he was doing, and how skilfully he managed the clever game he was playing: bringing home to Miss P. the small provincial corner she inhabited, a rabbit-hole in his scheme of things and in his estimation.

Even the old lady was moved to a gentle reproof when they next met:

'You were not at your best — not at your best,' she said.

Roseudgeon himself was pleased at having given Miss P. her comeuppance at last — after the persecution he considered he had endured over the years.

Earlier on he knew two or three women in her condition and class, spinsters on edge to get married.

'What is it that women really want?', the old princess had once discussed with her husband. 'Is it rank and title? Is it sex?

A handsome man, well endowed, with good prospects? The promise of a good life, good times together, similar tastes, etc?'

In the end, they both concluded that what women wanted more than anything was — Money.

The writer in Roseudgeon was more broad-minded, and was willing to broaden the conception.

He considered that what women wanted most was — Security. Money was an expression of it, rather a condition of it.

Thinking over the unsatisfied lives those two or three women lived in their fancied superior station, he wondered why they did not settle for an upstanding, well-equipped farmer ready to hand. (In their situation *he* would have done.) Only one woman in that class did he know of who had made that option: married her farmer — and been cut off by her (county) family in consequence.

What nonsense to sacrifice one's happiness to rank, he thought, himself having none.

Reflecting over the story of his relations with Miss P., he had known all along that marrying her would have been fatal: a chain-smoker — and he detested smoking, especially in women. Miss P. occasionally rang him up when a bit tiddly in the evening. Himself disliked drink — and remembered that Byron had not liked seeing women even eating.

But Roseudgeon had made one mistake about Miss Pengrugla. Acutely aware of differences of class, he had earlier thought of her, and dismissed her, as middle class. She was not: she was an accepted figure in the county. She was a lady — and he was not a gentleman.

V

Who was Miss Flavell?

At the corner of the street leading up to the Castle at Carlisle —
whence Mary Queen of Scots once looked out on a game played
between Scots and English on the Debateable Land — stood a
little chemist's shop in the early years of Queen Victoria. Above
it was inscribed, in slightly foreign lettering, 'M.C.J. Flavell.
Chymist and Apothecary.'

What an odd name thought any passer-by in coach or
barouche, phaeton or victoria, whose eye was caught by it.

The townsfolk were used to it, though Chemist Flavell was
indeed of foreign stock, his parents — understood to have been
of good class — having been *émigrés* from the French Revolution. Some of them assumed that the 'M' in the lettering stood
for 'Monsieur', but in the usual incurious way of humans, never
found out.

One day in those years there drove up to the door a large,
lumbering, but private, coach, out of which stepped a grand
lady — townsfolk did not know how grand, for indeed she was a
lady of the Royal Court.

The unknown lady was handed out, stepped inside the shop,
but was conducted into the private premises at the back.

There ensued a consultation of some duration, at the end of
which the lady was ushered out with ceremony to her coach.
The vehicle was then driven out of the city, northwards across
the Borders and into the Highlands, who knows whither?

Not long after there appeared in the Flavell family a girl, of
some delicacy of deportment and complexion. She was indeed
not strong, and the family kept much to themselves. The townsfolk saw little of her and knew less; she was simply spoken of,
with respect, as Miss Flavell — no other appellation, or Christian
name given.

In the bosom of that somewhat reserved, respected family she remained a few years, passing from girlhood into a not particularly blooming maidenhood, for she remained delicate.

Then one day, when approaching her majority, in those days at eighteen for women, a coach arrived as before, but southward bound. She was carried away south, to be seen and heard of no more in remote Carlisle.

It happened that a gentleman of ancient family in those parts was decidedly musical, and thus became acquainted with Mendelssohn in the musical life of London. It is well known that Mendelssohn was regarded with great favour by the Prince Consort and Queen Victoria, with their pure German tastes.

Thus it was that our Cumbrian gentleman, a Mr Settlethwaite, became a friend of the organist at Windsor, and from time to time, on his journeys south, would stay with him in his pretty little house in the Cloisters.

There one day he met Miss Flavell, who shared their musical interests and would take part in pianoforte duets of an afternoon in those delectable precincts.

She was now a lady in middle age, still very retiring, and not much known outside that circle. She had a little house on the edge of the Great Park. And there Mr Settlethwaite would occasionally visit this mysterious lady with her withdrawn, somewhat hieratic, manner — so far removed from the Chemist's shop at Carlisle.

He could not but wonder; but, nature's gentleman, he would not pry, and made no inquiries as to how she became removed from Carlisle to Windsor, of all places. No one volunteered any information: in those sacred precincts they knew better — as much as their job was worth.

They knew just what was known to the public — that George III was particularly fond of Windsor, and had made the old Granville lady, Mrs Delany, comfortable in a little house near the Castle, where he and Queen Charlotte could go and call on her. The old King had regarded himself as a townsman there, and would call in at the bookshops — he was the greatest book-collector of the age (apart from Richard Heber, with whose private life that of the philopregenitive George III was in much contrast). All the Hanoverian family were musical, with a special devotion to Handel, whom they regarded as practically their private possession. And George IV had rebuilt the inner court of the Castle, which contained the Royal apartments, as well as creating his pleasure-dome, the Pavilion at Brighton.

Mr Settlethwaite could not but notice, on his infrequent visits to Miss Flavell, an exotic object in her entrance hall: a Chinese lantern such as might have come from the Pavilion, or from the Chinese Room at Carlton House, long since dismantled.

One day the ageing lady herself showed him an engaging object, which George IV had presented to his Egeria, the Marchioness of Conyngham. Ladies had a name for it — a hold-all, or what?: a little work-basket of morocco and red velvet in which were stuck all that a lady would need for embroidery — needles, scissors, thimbles, bodkins. But all of gold.

On another occasion a book lay open, with the bookplate of the Queen's father, the Duke of Kent. Everybody knew that the Duke had lived happily for many years with the charming Frenchwoman, Madame de St Laurent — so charming that the Royals took her to themselves and were on friendly terms with her.

Unlike the Duke of Clarence with Mrs Jordan and their mass of children, Kent and his mistress had no offspring, it was thought. And on the Princess Charlotte's unexpected death, the Duke had had to marry hurriedly to provide an heir to the throne. He had provided an heiress, the young Victoria; then incontinently died himself.

It was less well known that Kent had been, like his father, a book collector. Here, lying open on the table, was a book of his with his fine book-plate. What was it doing here?

Mr Settlethwaite could not but notice in the old lady's boudoir a couple of engravings of Herrenhausen, the country palace of the Hanover family, with its famous breed of white horses. At the accession of Queen Victoria Hanover, of course, had come to the unpopular Duke of Cumberland by the rule of male succession that prevailed in that German kingdom.

But what were all these Hanoverian possessions doing in this

quiet, retired little house on the edge of Windsor Great Park? —
The old lady appeared to be surrounded by them.

On Mr Settlethwaite's last visit to Miss Flavell, she said to him,
without emotion or any self-pity:

'My physician tells me that I have not long to live. I should
like you to have something as a keepsake, to remind you of our
long acquaintance.'

What she handed to him was a quite large silver snuff-box,
with the monogram of George IV as Prince Regent, and the
triple-feathers as Prince of Wales. Inside was not a card but a
piece of her own writing-paper with its Windsor heading, and in
her shaky hand, simply 'Miss Flavell'. Perhaps it had long been
there, for the year was now well on in the reign of Queen Victoria.

Cumberland's son and heir was deprived of his kingdom of
Hanover by the Prussians, but retained his English title as Duke
and kept up his affiliations with this country. He sent his son
briefly to Oxford, where Mr Settlethwaite's son and heir was
awarded the privilege of keeping an eye on the young
Hanoverian princeling.

This was rightly (and royally) appreciated. On a later visit to
this country, the ex-King, but Duke, paid a call on Mr Settlethwaite junior. His eye caught the Prince Regent's gleaming
snuff-box, proudly displayed in a place of honour. Opening it
he read Miss Flavell's name on her slip of paper.

At once his manner changed, from courteous to quite fierce.
He barked brusquely:

'What do *you* know about Miss Flavell?'

The Englishman was quite taken aback by the outburst — as if
his most prized possession had been stolen. He flushed.

Upon this, the Duke calmed down, and said peaceably:

'Well, it was Prinny's all right.'

No more was said, and he took his leave.

It gave the young Settlethwaite furiously to think — though he
did not know *what* to think, for his father had told him no more
— perhaps knew no more, though he may have made a surmise
and, being a discreet man, kept it to himself.

VI

Hotel Bedroom in War Time

'Male and female created He them'
Genesis, 1. 27

The misanthropical man verging on middle age, though not yet forty, came up at the end of the evening from the hotel lounge, that buzzing hive of personal relations, feeling — as he often did nowadays — a little lonely. He lapsed into the one armchair by the dressing table; immediately behind him, the locked door communicating with the next room.

Drowsing for a while, he was brought to an alert by the arrival of voices behind the door.

'You let me down. You're always letting me down. You're no use as a husband. You don't know how to be one.'

It was the voice of a girl, small, suppressed, but vibrant with anger and contempt.

'But — darling — what have I done now?'

It was the surprised voice, amiable and of an attractive masculine timbre, of a young fellow who had had a little, but not a great deal, too much to drink. Definitely Public School. Both of them rather upper-class, or upper middle class — at any rate, good class — and very young.

'You never got rid of Bobby and Mick, but kept them hanging on, in spite of my giving you a look.'

A low and rapid fire of charges against him rattled off like a diminutive machine-gun. It made it hard for the listener, now all ears to make out what she had against him.

It seemed to be no less hard for the young man to make out what she was accusing him of.

This elicited a movement of sympathy, even a fellow-feeling, in the not quite hardened heart of the misanthrope (but was he really a misanthrope? Perhaps not altogether), and a certain response to the fresh young male voice, ardent and flustered. He saw him as hardly more than a boy — but married, poor young fellow.

'Yes, I did,' he was protesting. 'I got rid of them most efficiently. If Mick stayed on a bit later, it wasn't my fault. I did my best. I never saw you looking at me. If you wanted me to get rid of him, you should have told me.'

The young man was no logician. He made up for want of logic by repeating his phrases over and over. Evidently not a clever young man, there was something charming in the innocent voice, fresh and boyish and direct: no guile.

'You should have told me. I'd do anything you wanted me to do. Yes, I would. I wouldn't do anything to annoy you in the world. You know I wouldn't. I didn't want him to stay. I only wanted to be with you.'

This lost him a little sympathy with the acute listener, upon whose ear a man abasing himself to a woman did not strike a welcome note. (Perhaps he was a misogynist, after all, rather than a misanthrope?)

Nor did the young fellow's propitiation of his wife do him any good. There was a fierce, low hiss of denial — evidently she was a little bitch, perhaps a snake. The listener saw her as something small, with her tiny voice, curled up, coiled, ready to strike, quite willing to wound.

They were both undressing rapidly, angrily, but eager to get into bed. The girl easily won the game. There was a slipping off of some silky material, with a hiss, and she was in bed.

He was left at the wash-basin nearby, braces flapping against his legs, brushing his teeth with vehemence, protesting all the time.

'What is this you've got against me, Janet? There's something more behind it than this. What is it you've got against me? Tell me what it is.'

From the other side of the room came a low hiss.

'Everybody knows you're hyssterical. Your whole family's hyssterical. Look how hyssterical you are now.'

'Hysterical, am I? So that's it. I'm hysterical. And who told you I was hysterical?'

No reply.

It did not sound to the listener that he was at all hysterical, but there was a note of concern in his voice.

'Janet, I want to know. I want to get to the bottom of this. Who was it who said I was hysterical?'

'The matron at the nursing-home said that the whole family was.' The little voice came ice-cold and clear, deliberately taunting.

'The nursing home' — had they already had a child? reflected the listener, misanthropy returning.

'So the matron at the nursing-home,' he repeated, like a schoolboy learning his lesson. 'What did the matron at the nursing-home in Edinburgh say?'

No reply. More concern in his voice.

'I must get to the bottom of this. You have something against me, and you won't tell me what it is. I'm telling you everything that's in my mind, and you won't tell me what's in yours.'

Masculine candour v. feminine lack of it, registered the misogynist. Male simplicity and directness; female duplicity and deviousness.

'Why am I hysterical? I ask you what the matron of the nursing home said, and you won't reply.'

He, and the listener, were wrong.

'She said' — the reply came slowly and tauntingly — 'she said that you were all, that the family was — well, *odd*.'

'So that's it. So I'm hysterical. Why am I hysterical? I must know. I must get to the bottom of this.'

'Well, look at you now. Aren't you being hysterical now?'

If he were hysterical now, the little voice, boring into him like a gimlet, was driving him into it. This is the way women get themselves murdered, reflected the listener, with a spurt of hatred for the little snake, curled up.

'I'm not the least bit hysterical. I'm perfectly calm. But if I were, that's because I know better than you what the danger is. Hull has been blitzed twice in this past week, and quite a lot of people have been killed.'

'Well, it doesn't do any good thinking about it. Just forget about it. Don't think about it.'

'I can't help thinking about it. I know what it means. You've never been in a real blitz. Just that couple of bombs in Edinburgh, and that's all you know about it. I've been through it, and I don't mind saying—'

'Exactly. You're hysterical' came the taunting little voice from the bed. Sharper than he was, she had led him on to this. She regarded her point as proved, and did not bother to speak again.

Clearly she despised him. The listener wondered whether this was deliberately planned to break with him. The young fellow seemed to have no such suspicion, but went on, with bull-like persistency, doggedly:

'I was six weeks in Chelsea through all the worst blitzes. You don't know how I behaved. You don't know if I was hysterical.'

She kept silence.

He finished undressing, turned out the light, went to the window to draw back the black-out and let in the air. The voice of the station-announcer echoed through the bombed aisles of the railway-station and in the empty chambers of the heart.

*

'Jenny, darling,' he said softly. 'There's something behind this. What is it you've got against me? I'm telling you everything that's in my mind, and you won't tell me what's in yours.'

'Jenny?' he said beseechingly.

A low murmur came from the other bed.

He had not got into bed with her. The *voyeur* – or should there not be a word *auditeur*? – was disappointed.

'So that's it. You've been holding that against me all this time. I admit I was drunk. But you *forgave* me!'

It was suddenly the voice of a boy. He went down a peg or two in the estimation of the auditor, not well pleased at one of his sex humiliating himself to a woman.

'That was last November – months ago. And now it's July – months afterwards – and you've been holding that at the back of your mind all this time against me. And besides, you *forgave* me, Jenny, have you forgotten?'

No reply. His voice, from being that of a boy, innocent and surprised, became that of a man.

'I've told you everything that's in my mind. You know I love you, that I've never loved anybody but you, that I always have and I always shall. I don't want anybody but you – and you hold something against me at the back of your mind all this time. If only you'd tell me when I am doing something that annoys you. You know I wouldn't do anything in the world, not consciously, to annoy you, Jenny darling.'

The misogynist was displeased. *He* would do something to annoy her, all right. He'd put the little creature in her place.

'You let me go on, never saying anything, and then, all of a sudden, you kick like this. Why don't you tell me?'

A sigh came from the other bed, with something like, 'It's no use.'

'But it *is*,' said the male, now a boy again. 'You don't know what influence you have over me, if only you would choose to exert it. I'd do anything you want me to do, if only you'd tell me. But you won't. You just let me go on, and then pull up short like this.'

He went down a little further. A riding type evidently, the auditor saw him as rather a fine-looking fellow, spare and athletic, direct and guileless, going straight for his fences. He was very much in love with her.

'I know I'm not clever like you. I don't pretend to be. But that's all the more reason why you should exert your influence. You've no idea what you can do with me.'

No reply. The silence itself spoke for her.

He now took a different line of appeal.

'Haven't you the imagination to see the thing from my point of view? You don't know how bloody awful this life in the Army is. You know how I hate it, not having any home to go to. It usen't to be like this, when we were in Edinburgh together. We were happy then. Now it's bloody awful, having these rows. Have a little imagination for me, Jenny – think of it from my point of view.'

He waited in the heart-beating darkness. Still no reply. The listener's heart was touched. For the first time in his life *he* wanted to say to a woman, 'Have a heart! Can't you see? His life is miserable. And he's in love with you.'

If only he were in love with *him*! But ordinary humans are not made that way.

A desolating sense of their youth came over the man who saw life from the outside: two children losing hold of each other, drifting apart upon the dark waters of the world, when so little an effort would keep them together, save them from shipwreck.

They seemed so young, and foolish, drifting on to the rocks, in the squalor of an hotel bedroom, when only a word from her, a gesture, would put it right so easily. *She* could have him at her feet, with just a word.

The unknown man was resentful at the thought, a double resentment — for the young soldier and for himself, for the very condition of life.

She would not say the word. The young husband waited in vain. There was a determined silence, an obstinate, hostile silence, which made itself felt in the room.

He had humbled himself to no purpose. His pride as a man revolted.

'Very well. You talk about my being no use as a husband. What about you as a wife? You don't come up to my idea of a wife. You think because you can write down little bits of nonsense on a bit of paper in the hope that it'll make a book that you're God Almighty. I don't think so. I know what I ought to do: I ought to take and smack you on the bottom until you were in a more sensible frame of mind.'

He got into his own bed. There was dead silence in the room.

*

Time passed. In the heart-beats of the listener it seemed an age.

When the young soldier spoke again he was in another mood: his voice was low and soft and appealing. Did he want to go to bed with the little creature?

'Jenny, darling,' he said.

There was not a sound. The hollow vacancy spoke.

'Jenny — do you realise that we've been married three years, and that we've never had a row before without making it up before going to sleep?'

There was the softness of desire in his voice, along with a new note, a deeper one, a note of reflection. He was thinking it over.

'Well, I suppose there's a train tomorrow that will take you back to Edinburgh, and I can go back to camp.'

(Tomorrow was a Sunday.)

'D'you know if there is a train?'

A short, crisp murmur from the other bed.

'I grant that you're a hard worker and that you can look after yourself. I hand it out to you for that. I admire you for it. No: I don't want to touch that two hundred a year, or whatever it is you've got. I don't want to hear of it — that's all yours.'

Silence.

When he spoke again it was with still greater softness.

'Jenny, won't you come half-way to meet me? It's never been like this before. Do you know, this is the first time that we've never made it up before going to sleep?'

The silence was full of meaning, baleful, intolerable. Evidently the little creature had made up her mind.

'Jenny, darling — you realise what this means?' — he spoke slowly, deliberately.

No answer — she made it felt that she knew perfectly well, and that she willed it so.

'Very well,' he said resignedly. He accepted the decision, 'I suppose we shall join the countless hundreds of other people who haven't made a success of marriage.'

*

The voice of the station-announcer echoed lugubriously under the wrecked roofs of the bombed railway-station. The outsider sat on stiff and cold in his chair, numbed by that close look into the very hearts of other human beings for which he hungered, himself for ever outside. This was what it was to be inside.

He did not sleep till morning, and rose late. Next morning the young couple had already gone from their room, left on their separate ways.

Coming upon their story years after, he wondered if the young soldier survived the war. He felt no concern about the little creature who was capable of looking after herself. Nor did he suppose that her book ever came to anything — though she came into his.

VII

Polly of Trethurgy

What's in a name? It is curious the difference just one consonant will make: between P and M, for instance. Molly suggests something soft and yielding — as in 'mollify' or 'emollient', hence 'molly-cuddle', I suppose. Not so with Polly: the word itself suggests personality, someone downright, 'all there', as we say — perhaps someone of power. It also suggests something familiar in the personality — as was the case in Polly's remarkable story: she *stood out*, was a character in our local scene.

She was born and bred at Trethurgy. That name means something too: tre-thur-gy means the village of the water dog, i.e. otter. So there must have been otters in old days in the stream that runs from that high-up, hard-bitten granite settlement on the moor down to the sea at Par.

She came from a respectable, religious-minded family: the old couple, her parents, used to hold services in their house before the little chapel was built at Bethesda. They had two children, Polly and a good-looking son — both above average village intelligence. The son, destined for the ministry, was going to Shebbeare College, that Stonyhurst of West Country Methodists. Polly became schoolmistress of the little Infants' School, in sole command, time on her hands.

Mr Benton was the School Attendance Officer, in those days when sending children to school every day was not regularly accepted by the country people and farming folk who had something better for them to do, needed them about the place.

Mr Benton — people called him 'Mr' respectfully out of deference for his job — was a fine-looking fellow. Anybody could see from his later, seedy days that he had more sex on him than he knew what to do with. He already had five kids, and his wife didn't want any more. So he played round with Polly.

In those days what else was there to do?

No wireless or television to occupy them. People were poor and hardly travelled outside their parishes. Evenings were long in winter — no electric light. Sex was all-in-all. By the same token randy young people had no notion of birth control — nor their elders either, unless they were religious people like Polly's parents.

She was not: she had a mind of her own.

Mr Benton had a wonderful copper-plate hand, people said, and a good head for accounts. Once a week he used to help Mr Kellow to balance accounts at his busy shop further down the hill — centre, along with Chapel, of the little community's intense, enclosed life, where everybody knew everything about everybody.

Thus Mr Benton's job gained him regular entrance into the Infants' School, and not only the school.

Soon the rumour flew round that Polly was sick. And then that Polly was going to have a baby.

'They say that I'm going to have a baby, Mrs Kellow,' Polly said firmly at that news centre; 'but I'm *not*.'

How was she so sure?

Mrs Endean, who did the village washing, knew better. She was a rough character with an edge to her tongue; she made up a lot of verses about Polly, and put them about.

Was she envious of Polly and the superior young School Attendance Officer she was so thick with?

People would say, 'How do you know so much about Polly, that she's going to have a baby, when she do deny it?'

Mrs Endean had her answer ready:

'I know it: I recognise the pattern of the crochet on her drawers.'

She was right. It became evident that Polly *was* going to have a baby. When she couldn't deny it any longer, she named Mr Benton as the father.

*

She left home and went away to Plymouth to have her child.

Polly maintained herself by keeping the accounts in a shop —
not everybody could do that in those days — and boarded out
the kid, a daughter.

Interest in the situation flagged. It had taken its normal
course — quite the usual thing in a Cornish village at the period:
the time of popular King Edward, himself not averse to such
goings-on. Good old Edwardian days and ways.

Then interest arose again, for the rumour came out that
there was going to be a maintenance case: Polly was to bring a
charge against Mr Benton to maintain his child. There was.

Mr Benton, however, had two friends who were powers in our
little land. His brother-in-law was Chairman of the Board of
School Managers, and his mate, who happened to be churchwarden, was also interested in education. They put their heads
together, got down a grand KC to defend Mr Benton, and got
him off.

Polly lost her case. It had all been a mistake, and left a mess.
For observe the consequences that flowed from it, in every direction — and in the years to come.

For Mr Benton first. Though technically he was whitewashed, neither his own family nor his conscience whitewashed
him. Nor did local people, for all that his friends and their fine
lawyer had done for him: the community was not taken in.

His wife and children were up in arms against him, and
would not have him in the house. Homeless, he had to find lodgings for himself.

His own conscience gnawed at him: he knew that he had
wronged Polly — doubly in defeating her case.

And what was he to do with all that sex?

He took to drink, like others in that case. From being the
popular likable fellow he had been, he became rather a bad lot,
consorting with other bad lots in the pubs in the town: a local
character, an Ishmael.

The local historian as a growing boy, upon whom little was
lost, would see him in his aunt's little shop occasionally of a
Saturday night, sitting himself down on the one rickety chair
not big enough for his broad behind, against a build-up of
unsteady biscuit tins.

He didn't want to buy anything, except perhaps a box of matches for an excuse to stay, while he filled his pipe again and again, squatting there large as life in a cloud of smoke. His money had gone on drink; he was already tiddly, fine blue eyes glazed and beery, smelling of drink and tobacco.

He was rather well dressed in a slack way, always tweeds like a sporting gentleman gone to seed. What he wanted was sympathy — sounding maudlin: 'I've no home to go to.'

'T'es 'is own fault,' said the unsympathetic aunt.

The leer with which he looked on the buxom woman who kept the shop was not lost on an observant lad. No sympathy in that quarter. 'Old Benton', as the boy called him, had no respect for women: he knew they were all flesh and blood.

What the boy did not know — and Benton did — was that his aunt, for all her hoity-toity airs, had had the same mischance as Polly. When another unmarried girl in the village got into trouble, he overheard his aunt say to the mother,

"Es, I knaw what 'tes like.'

He thought this was sympathy; he did not know that it was just identifying, self-sympathy, in the way of ordinary humans — though he already thought that grown-ups were fools.

A sensitive boy, he shared his aunt's disgust with the large mass of smelly humanity occupying so much space in the little shop. He noticed that his uncle was more kindly disposed — perhaps a bond of male sympathy with the old reprobate, as against the freemasonry of women. It was the women who had it in for 'Old Benton' — the respectable ones putting up their show of morality. Society needs the cement of decorum to keep it together, or, in another word, humbug.

*

And what, meanwhile, of Polly?

She sent her little girl, Irene — hardly suitably named, no peace-offering, no eirenicon — home to her father and mother to be brought up as theirs. To the child she was always 'Auntie Polly' — a caption so common in Cornwall as almost to regularise such situations.

Polly got herself a better job, again keeping accounts, in a big butcher's shop in London. When her little girl was about five or six, Polly gave herself a holiday, and at last came home. Arriving at our station, she took a closed cab up the steep hill to Trethurgy.

After that first time it came easier to her to come home again and walk down through the village as of old.

Eventually she came back to Cornwall with a job, again as a schoolmistress, somewhere way down by the Lizard. All the while Irene was growing up, Polly was doing quite well on her own — careful, not only not to make any more slips, but financially. She always had a good head for accounts, had taken out two or three insurance policies, and been thrifty.

As Polly said herself, she had been lucky. She built the substantial big house where Irene came to live, and two, if not three, bungalows besides.

But her daughter never knew that Polly was her mother until her own wedding day, when she had to be told. She took it very badly.

'To think I have been deceived all my life until my own wedding,' she said.

She would never forgive it, nor recognise her mother, or speak to her.

Nor did she, though she lived in the house her mother had provided for her, with her mother next door.

Irene was a throw-back to her grandparents, religious and upright: she would not recognise the facts and continued to regard the old people as having been her parents.

Irene has a son, who turns after her and them — rather stuck up — 'bigoty' is the Cornish word for it. When Polly died the other day, she left the house and all her property direct to him.

*

And 'Old Benton's' family?

The eldest daughter, Julia — so proudly named — who had disapproved of her father when a girl, turned out as strongly sexed as he was. She made a career as a high-class tart in

Devonport — plenty of custom there, hers among the upper decks rather than the lower. She prospered and held her head as high as Irene. Humbug has different ways its wonders to perform.

VIII

The Fan

I

As a writer he received a good deal of fan-mail. Most of it could
safely be ignored and, like E. M. Forster, his 'patience with
ordinary people was giving out.' Anyway, he didn't depend on
his novels for a livelihood; they were a sideline. He had a more
secure base of subsistence as a County official, and had come to
be recognised as an authority on its history, the repository of its
folklore, particularly of his native parish.

One day he received a letter from a far-away town in the
North Country that gave him pause.

'I have been reading your biography', an unknown woman
wrote — meaning autobiography, as people usually did, not
knowing the difference.

'I feel sure that you are the only person that can help me. I
am a married woman with two children growing up, and
happily married I may say. I am Cornish and feel deeply
Cornish, and know that my mother came from there. But I
never knew my mother — I only know that I was illegitimate,
and I have never been to Cornwall. I long to see Cornwall
with a passionate longing I can hardly explain. My husband
cannot understand it; he is a solid North Countryman. He
thinks I am crazy. I write to you because I have read your
book and feel that you will understand it and sympathise. I
have a double longing to see and know where I belong,
where my mother came from — I know nothing about my
father or who he was. Can you tell me something about my
mother's people who cast her off? I have never been able to

get in touch with them, or find out. Are they all dead, or what? I long to know.'

*

As a matter of fact, the county official — novelist and folklorist in his spare time — *did* know, for the woman gave the mother's name. He was one of the very few people alive who knew the family story.

It made a cruel scandal so many years ago, though even then hushed up as far as possible, the actors in it at once dispersed — and few there were that remembered. The second German war had intervened, the district filled up with incoming 'foreigners'. Would there be anyone else who knew the story?

He at once realised that it would be too cruel to tell the unknown woman what perhaps he alone, faithful to the past, knew.

He contented himself with a letter of consoling generalities — that her people were a much respected family of good local standing — as in fact they had been. The Treglowns had been millers for several generations, had owned their flour-mill down in the valley below the little church-town that had expanded unrecognisably since the war.

Old townspeople knew the family for what they were: comfortably well-to-do; when local flour-milling was coming to an end, they sold their business well to a big combine, and were able to retire on the proceeds. The folklorist remembered that the old bachelor brother of the head of the family had a fine collection of china he had put together — early Cookworthy, Plymouth and Bristol; Staffordshire figures of John Wesley — for the family were leading members of the Methodist chapel in the town.

(What had happened to that treasure, in the long years since and the old boy had died, he wondered? *That* he did not know.)

*

Many months passed, perhaps a year, and there came another letter, more pressing than before.

Did the poor woman suspect that he was holding something

back, that he knew more than he was willing to tell her? Had he known her mother?

To this he was able to answer truthfully that he had not. He had not even known the family, only knew of them as much respected, good old townsfolk of many generations in the place. Himself a local recorder, he knew that the Treglowns had been among the first converts and followers of John Wesley, who had preached from the steps of their dwelling in the Fore Street. They had taken a leading part in building the big Wesleyan Chapel, now glorified under the name of St John's Church.

Did this satisfy her? Would this head her off?

Perhaps it was not to be expected that it would.

An interval of some months elapsed when she wrote again.

Could he tell her nothing about her mother? She had not even a photograph of her.

'I long to know what she looked like, whether I or my two girls take after her. We are a happy family in ourselves, my husband is good to me. But he cannot understand that I cannot be contented until I know about myself and where I come from. I feel from your book that you are the only person who can understand that.'

To this she added what she did know — that her mother had so disgraced the family that she had been sent away from home, her child put out to nurse, provided for in a home, so that she had never known her, only the name she had disgraced.

The writer was genuinely sympathetic in his reply — told her that she should not think in such terms. People nowadays did not think of such things as a 'disgrace', one should think of the gift of life as a blessing, something to be grateful for, however one came into the world, etc, etc.

(He did not say that he had enough skeletons in his own family cupboard to be able to understand her complex — for complex it undoubtedly was.)

For yet another letter came after more months had passed.

'I cannot explain why it is that I have this longing to see the place I come from, that I have never seen. We are working people, and I have never had the money or the time, with my family to look after and bring up, to go all the way to Cornwall. Yet I feel so drawn to it, as if by a *double* pull. Was my father Cornish too? I imagine so — though I know nothing about him, nor who he was, not even his name. And I do not suppose you know, any more than I know any of my relatives who cast my mother off and broke off all relations. Are any of them alive? Sometime I think I shall try and make the journey and come to Cornwall, the feeling is so deep in me, and nobody understands. Perhaps you will help me.'

At this he took fright. He had heard of authors who had had to take evasive action from the pursuit of too ardent fans. Hadn't Walt Whitman felt obliged to abscond to Philadelphia when a passionate English admirer threatened to descend on him in New York? Hadn't Gide felt the necessity to *s'évader* to avoid the visits of the Strachey woman, Mme Bussy?

Nothing in the correspondence so far indicated that his fan was a pest of this sort or had that kind of interest in him. Still, one never knew . . . better to disengage and drop the correspondence. In any case he could not tell her what he knew.

He did not reply.

II

When he was a boy the head of the Treglown family had been something of a public figure, well enough known locally by his first names, 'Walter John'. The leading light of the Methodist Chapel, he alternated as Chairman of the Urban District Council, turn and turnabout, with the Church of England churchwarden, old, bearded Sidney Hewas.

Where the latter was a short-tempered, irascible figure, with an easily aroused angry gleam behind his spectacles, Walter John, less burly and less bearded, was more benign, and consequently popular. Also more easy-going than his colleague, and so surpassed him in the number of times they chaired the

Council, chain on ample chest, some six to five in those innocent days before the end of the old civilisation was announced on 4th August 1914.

Walter John's hopeful son, Walter, had joined up early in the Yeomanry, had good luck, and came home unscathed from the war, as many did not. So also his sister, Ellen, a rather mannish girl, who made a successful land-girl and did good work on the farms to which she was recruited.

What to do with them when they returned from the war?

There was a good deal of unemployment, and many emigrated from the district.

This was not to the mind of Walter and Ellen, who had both been away throughout the war and were longing to get back and be settled in their native home to which they were deeply attached. It was in their blood — of generations going back beyond remembrance.

Walter had the easy-going nature of his father; his sister inherited more of the drive that had made the success of the flour-mills in previous generations. The brother had no particular inkling as to what he wanted to do on coming out of the army; it was his sister, a favourite with their father, who clinched the matter with him. They would farm, and make a go of it together.

A neat little farm was bought for them, on the outskirts of the town, on the lower slopes of the downs. The upper half of it rough pasture, the lower half arable, which gave the curious name of Phernyssick Farm to the whole.

The writer — no Celtic scholar, for all his knowledge of local lore — could not be sure what it meant. He knew that 'issick' meant cornfield; but what did 'Pher' mean: was it the old Cornish for 'road' — the road by the cornfield?

From his boyhood he had always known of the secret spring there, which gave the purest, iciest water when supplies ran short in the village below and he would take a large earthenware pitcher to the gully where the spring never failed, coming from the bowels of the great heave of hill above.

Somehow, for all its bare, gaunt stoniness there was a strong sexuality about that landscape. Whatever gave it its suggestiveness? It was the reverse of lush: it was harsh and abrupt, great rocks like half-submerged monsters sticking up out of the short turf, exposing themselves to sun and moon. To him it had all the sexuality that Egdon Heath had for Hardy.

Was it that half the population of the village below had been conceived up here in the shelter of the furze bushes on hot summer nights?

Half way up stood out from the cluster of houses their Bethesda Chapel, where the boys and girls, in those innocent days, eyed each other — then there was Look-out Lane, where girls not on the look-out got pregnant in the spring.

For the writer himself there was a more vivid, if recondite, association that went right back to his early childhood: a blood-red blind of a cottage window behind which he learned that a woman had died in childbirth. The strange thing was that this gave him his first intimation of sexual excitement, though no more than a child.

*

The farmhouse at Phernyssick was a little granite cottage, in a hollow, as secret as the spring. It was indeed extraordinarily sequestered, hidden away from prying eyes. No one knew what went on there, for they employed no labour — no need to on such a small holding. Ellen not only did the housework but gave a hand with the cattle. They had half-a-dozen Jerseys, which thrive on such sweet short-turfed grass salted with sea-air, tang of camomile and what all.

In the cottage itself there was hardly room to fling a cat about — not that either of them would have thought of it. Animals are we all and, like animals, are conceived, are born and die. It is just that our lives have lost innocence — as Adam and Eve found (were they not brother and sister?) — and are more troubled by the knowledge of Good and Evil.

Brother and sister lived together in the closest proximity in their Garden of Eden. Who took the first step?

It is to be surmised that Ellen did: she had the drive, the energy: she really ran the farm — and her brother. The word that went round for Walter was that he was 'lackadaisical'.

True enough. He was not one to think of consequences.

During his years away at the war he had had no responsibilities; he had only to obey commands, his but to do and die. Actually he had been lucky; he thought that his luck would always hold.

As the only boy in that good old family he had always been a bit spoiled — not least by his sister, a few years older, and the stronger, more aggressive character.

No one knew what went on in their little eyrie on the gaunt hillside; they held themselves aloof from the village below: they were in fact rather superior — townsfolk, more than a cut above the village people.

But the village had eyes — and tongues — and what went on became evident enough as Ellen's pregnancy became no longer concealable.

The scandal broke and raged for a time like a furze fire on the downs.

It was extinguished and hushed up as soon as possible. The young couple were separated and rushed away — no one knew whither — but at any rate before the arm of the law could reach them. It was only a few years before 1914 that the illiberal legislation of the Liberal government had made incest a severely punishable crime — months, years of imprisonment. Before that measure of 'progress' only a sin — familiar enough in lonely, constricted, overcrowded cottages — but not a crime, savagely punished.

Brother and sister were quickly spirited away: Walter to Africa, where he was lost sight of; Ellen 'up-country' to have her baby, where it was brought up in a home, and she shortly died.

There was even a worse consequence. The father, our 'Walter John' — all his life something of a public figure — could not face the public disgrace of his family and committed suicide, the local recorder never knew how.

After all, it had happened in his own early days. He never knew details of the anguish, the agony on all sides it entailed.

He recognised the well-known name of the local family that thus came to an end, and that his fan, so passionately anxious to know the facts about her background and how she came into the world, was the off-spring of a brother and sister.

It gave him food for thought. Was this the reason for her

insatiable longing for the native Cornwall in her blood, felt along her veins though she had never been there? Her double and redoubled infusion of blood that left her discontented at not knowing, perpetually gnawing at a life otherwise happy enough?

The writer never heard from his fan again. Was she dead? Or had she found some other way of knowing the story he could never tell her?

IX

The Rocking Horse

'You know,' said the Professor, in his authoritative way, laying down the law, 'to be intelligent is to be abnormal. It is not a normal thing for a family to throw up anyone really intelligent — only once in a while does that happen. The usual family bumbles along decently enough according to its station, one up, one down, no one particularly standing out.'

'What about the occasional appearance of a genius in the line?' asked his companion.

'Quite unaccountable. Nothing to do with the line, so far as we know. A mutation, a sport: a sudden leap, in the way evolution goes.'

'Well, what about a sudden descent, bringing the line to an end — at any rate ruin to the family?'

'That can happen too — in fact, does much more frequently. Especially in these appalling times of ours, with standards breaking down all round us. It was the strength of family tradition that kept ordinary folk on the rails. When that goes, there is nothing much in themselves to prop them up.'

'You see a pretty dismal outlook for our time, then?'

'Well, yes — good old stocks that played their part in building up the greatness of the nation faltering and failing; everywhere their country houses closing down, emptied of their contents — when, before 1914, this country was a treasure house of the world — splendid houses with their pictures, portraits, furniture, books, papers now dispersed, sold off to America. The houses destroyed in hundreds, when not turned into institutions, offices, flats.'

'Well, anything to keep the roof on.'

'Very often it isn't,' rejoined the Professor gloomily. Nothing relieved his gloom whenever he contemplated the times he lived in and the world around him. 'And the odd thing is that there seems an unaccountable incidence, even frequency of fires on top of all that − as if deliberately to bring things to an end. The Devil's in it, as folks hereabouts say.'

*

The hereabouts were a fertile parish on the edge of a West Country moor, practically all good arable land − which had been the foundation of an ancient family's prosperity. But, in addition, they owned mineral rights over an extent of the moor, which gave promise of considerable further wealth in time to come − with the discovery of china clay on their land and the prospect of its development.

Not that the family would take a hand in that: they had no business capacity and not much feeling for the valuable estate they had inherited. They were not West Country by origin, and for the last few generations were Army people living much abroad, particularly in India, where they had been Gurkha officers on the North-West Frontier, or Bengal Cavalry men. In one generation two or three of the infants had been born and baptized at Simla in the good old days.

In their tradition of Army service they also picked up their tradition of alcoholism: the last three baronets were confirmed alcoholics.

'I know I'm an alcoholic, and I don't mind,' said the last of them all − though he did not confess to something more and worse. He did not come clean about his drug addiction, which he had picked up in India.

Only his local doctor knew about that. The Professor was the doctor's son, and so knew the story of the family in its last generations before his own time. He was much less tolerant of its little idiosyncrasies: he hated waste − and they were extravagant, easy-going, generous too. One way and another they − or, rather, their sensible womenfolk − did a great deal of good in the parish. They were always handing out.

The baronets and the men of the family were much away from home − anyway they had a convenient house in London. Though they were all Army men, oddly enough the baronetcy went back to a handsome sailor — a gallant fellow who was second in command at Camperdown.

For service there he was baronetted and — more to the point — got the chief command at Plymouth. There he had picked up the West Country heiress — not much to look at, but desirable enough on account of her property — to whom they owed estate, house, and wealth, which went on increasing through the long Victorian prosperity.

The old house was not a liability, it had not been rebuilt on the grand scale like some of the Regency sham-castles which proved mill-stones round the necks of their later owners. The nucleus of it was an L-shaped Jacobean house, to which the Georgians had added a more shapely, regular wing. Long and low, rather rambling, it was a cosy place in its way — large stables behind for the hunters in which the family took pride and were to be seen chasing over the Moor with the hounds they kept.

'Another silly extravagance,' commented the censorious Professor.

*

It fell to his father, the Doctor, to dance attendance on Sir Godfrey, the last baronet, who made rather a friend of him, at least a crony. For the Doctor lived in the village, had not a large practice, and was expected to look in on the Baronet every day that he was in residence. He was here more on retirement from the Army, with the exalted rank of Captain of the — Rangers' Militia. Their regular jamborees gave more occasion for carousals and drinking in company, besides Sir Godfrey's solitary dedication to the bottle. Naturally, he had a well-stocked cellar, and the house in its last days overflowed with food and wine. There was a large household; the village lived by it — and partly off it.

The Doctor's son had no patience with any of it; but anyway he was much away from home at the university. As a high-brow of Leftist sympathies, he was not an intimate of the big house, had no wish to be, and had nothing in common with its inmates.

Nor was he fully apprised of the goings-on there and how closely involved his father was with its fate.

The Doctor had a kindly nature and a warm feeling for the good side in the Baronet's nature — his friendliness to all and sundry, his open-handedness. As a doctor he tried to do his best for his old friend, but there was little enough that he could do for him, except give him his company.

Nobody could do anything with, or for, Sir Godfrey: he was incorrigible. His mother had been Irish: perhaps she introduced the vein of mulish obstinacy into the stock, along with the generosity, the thoughtless extravagance.

The Doctor tried to get his old friend to reduce his drug allowance bit by bit. In vain, the Baronet had the addict's usual way of cheating, going behind the Doctor's back, in touch with the little North Devon port of Appledore through which supplies used then to come in.

The Doctor, fearing trouble, tried to persuade his eldering friend to give up his guns — he had long ceased to be any good as a shot around the estate. Game and vermin alike proliferated in the coverts: pheasant and partridges, plover up on the high Moor; also foxes and badgers. The foxes prowled round the house and predated upon the peacocks — those that hadn't learned to roost up above ground.

No hope: Sir Godfrey would not give up his guns.

His wife could do nothing with him either, and took herself off for long intervals to her native Scotland, without entirely giving him up or divesting herself of all interest in the place and its succession.

This threw the Baronet still more on his friend's resources. He would summon the Doctor up to a feed of ham and eggs at five o'clock in the morning — just when he felt like it.

The hefty meal would be brought up to Sir Godfrey's bedroom by his manservant, his batman from old Army days, who slept within call. The former Major would order him about in parade-ground manner, waking him up unconscionably at any hour.

The Doctor was always taken by the surprising feature that dominated the Baronet's bleak bedroom with hard iron camp-bed. This was a splendid great 18th century rocking-horse — spotted grey mare, coloured bridle, bright harness — upon which generations of children had rocked to and fro. As had the Baronet as a boy. It seemed the one thing that was nearest his vacant heart, for he kept it close to him and rested his bleared eyes fondly upon it when he could not sleep. It made a happy feature in his dreams.

*

He had always been used to having his own way, plenty of money in hand, never considering the consequences. Bored in London on his own, no chauffeur with him, he would command a taxi to drive him incontinent to his place in the West Country — a bill for £60, worth something in those days, meant nothing.

Once, in the earlier days of air-services, he went to the London airport to command a private aeroplane to take him to some regimental reunion in Malta — but found that this was not on.

He found himself increasingly frustrated, and at length, financially. He had never taken much interest in either his business or estate affairs — except to be good, in a casual, unconsidering way with his tenants. So he was always popular.

'Naturally, with fools,' thought the Professor; 'they never like sensible people who calculate ends according to their means, and cut their coat according to their cloth.'

When the world depression hit the country in 1931 Sir Godfrey didn't know what had hit him: the money that had always been at hand — his local bank manager positively obsequious to the Bart — simply wasn't there! How could this be?

Tenants of his farms couldn't pay their rents. The China-clay trade that had boomed after the First German War, sank into deep depression, shares fallen to zero — no return on them. (Those who had the good fortune to pick them up then eventually made a tremendous killing.)

Sir Godfrey was in despair. Not knowing where to turn, he turned to his 'estranged' wife.

She gallantly descended from Scotland to do what she could. And reasonably began operations by shortening staff. After this brief raid, reducing household expenses by a head, she departed, leaving Sir Godrey to it, more flustered than enlightened.

He felt the atmosphere somehow rendered uncomfortable.

Shortly afterwards, the old mansion went on fire.

Who, or what, was responsible?

The fire made a great sensation, visible for miles round. The house itself stood on the slope of a hill, and everybody, from the parish and its neighbour, ran to the rescue.

In the event quite a lot of the contents and valuables were saved, brought out and scattered around the large front lawn. A full length Romney of the heiress who had brought the place to the family – rather romanticised, if truth be told (thought the Professor). A more realistic Raeburn, which had come down in the wife's family (more to his taste, without illusions as to people or art). A couple of dullish Hudsons in the usual fancy dress, and a grim Northcote of that penny-saving, Plymouth painter.

The house, in the manner of old West Country mansions, had been dripping with good china – some of it Chinese armorial pieces made for the Western market, some *famille rose* and *famille verte*, and a lot of blue-and-white which had come in through Devon and Cornish ports.

Much of this was saved, lying in heaps upon the grass. The Baronet looked on in despair. ('Fat lot he knew or cared about it,' registered the Professor, who knew about these things and was resentful that he had not succeeded to such an inheritance: *he* would have known how to look after it – *he* was one of the exceptions in a family line.)

However, there was no saving the beautiful mahogany doors from Honduras, which the first Baronet had collected in his naval career and proudly installed in his wife's friendly old mansion.

*

But what had caused the conflagration?

The explanation that was put about was the usual, most common one: a wooden beam in an old chimney.

Those in the know knew better. It was the Baronet, they said, who, going down into the cellar in the early hours of the morning, had left a candle alight on the stairs, which caught the curtains afire.

He himself, in his alcoholic stupor and stunned by the event, didn't know whether that might not be so.

It was some years later that the truth came to the ears of the Doctor, who passed it on to his son.

The village always knows the truth in these matters, but are apt to keep it to themselves: no easy task for middle- or upper-class people to penetrate into their enclosed world. However, the Doctor was a privileged person.

In the course of her raid on the house the Baronet's wife made a discovery — one which was usual enough in country houses. A lot of food came into the house for the too-large household. The cook had her family and relations to provide for in the next-door parish. In the regular way of such she laid by provisions for them on an out-of-the-way shelf in the barn at the end of the stable-yard: quite a bit of left-overs from the dining-room, half-a-chicken or -boiled fowl, a quarter-ham or juicy bit of meat. The Baronet never noticed, hadn't much appetite anyway; he took his nourishment otherwise. To the left-overs the cook would add as much that was not left over: eggs, a bag of sugar or rice, a packet of tea, sometimes for a family occasion a cake of her own making.

How had this come to light?

It was not the right thing for the village, or even the parish, to betray one another. Most of the servants came from within the parish. The family had done many good things for the neighbourhood, one way or another; but the gentry were always fair game. Nobody told.

However, one of the kitchen servants came from the next-door parish. Cook had reckoned without proper parish-feeling. People in the parish of St A. couldn't abide people in the parish of St B. They had regular old-time folk insults for them: 'they built a wall to 'edge in the cuckoo'; 'they do knuckly down upon one knee' (to do what? Fie!).

The kitchenmaid from St B. split on the cook to the Mistress. Cook, a St A. woman, was sacked, the kitchenmaid promoted.

The cook took her revenge before she departed and set the house on fire.

How did the village know that?

Because it was noticed that, though most of the servants' clothes in their attics perished in the fire, the cook's were not up there: they had been moved in time to her hide-out in the barn.

*

The Baronet surveyed the scene of desolation, the house still smouldering, despair in his fuddled head. Quite a bit of the ancient part, stables and barn, still intact. Something could yet be made of it — but not by him.

When he at length saw his favourite rocking-horse brought out and stood firmly on its legs amid the heaps of crockery, pictures, furniture, he awoke to the sense of his misery: something at last broke in him.

That night he took his favourite gun and shot himself.

'A good riddance, the fool,' said the Professor, who had the strong-minded person's contempt for the weak.

The Doctor, more kindly disposed to human weakness — after all, it was his vocation, his own living, to care for it — even shed a tear at his old friend's funeral.

After the last Baronet's death, the whole estate was sold, the family there at an end.

'If only they had held on' . . . reflected the Professor, who had money-sense as well as sense, 'with the immense development of china-clay on the Moor, and all their mineral rights and royalties, today they would have been millionaires.'

X

Blue Waves

'Delightful seaside villa, southward looking coast of Cornwall, glorious view of bay and headland, maximum sun, minimum cost and care, easily run, help available as required.' This somewhat ambivalent advertisement caught the eye of a retiring (in both senses) couple, in 'the sodden and unkind' Midlands of Belloc's description. After inquiry as to price and the help available, they immediately settled on visiting and viewing it.

They considered themselves lucky in the sum for which they obtained it, some £8,000 or so; but prices were still variable and unsettled at the end of the war. It did not occur to them that the price was suspiciously low for the jewel they had got. To be sure, 'help' was vague and likely to be forthcoming only in the shape of assistance in the garden from the village over the heave of hill.

But the garden was not large and should not be troublesome to an eldering couple, with occasional help. It was a narrow downward-sloping strip between the lane to a cove and the cliff's edge. Along the wall that marked off the boundary of the property at the back ran a very narrow path to a little bluff, which looked directly, perpendicularly upon the rocks below.

The house did not in fact face the south, as the advertisement seemed to suggest, but south-west − and in consequence got the full beat of the dominant south-westerly gales. Nor did the new occupants have much reason to appreciate the villa's somewhat optimistic name. Rarely were the waves ever blue: they were almost always grey or a murky green, the further headland often either wrapped in, or obscured by, mist, an indistinct, somewhat threatening shape. Or, rather, it assumed differing shapes, reptilian like lizard or turtle, sometimes suggesting something human, which was worse.

They found that the bluff practically at their backdoor – one would have to be careful not to prowl in the dark, one might tumble, or be tumbled, over – had a name: Carrickhowel on the map. Local people did not use it. Why ever not? The newcomers rather fancied it, thought it sounded romantic, and asked their gardening-help what it meant.

He was no help in this direction. Cornish folk had long ago lost the meanings of their place names. Looking up words in a Cornish dictionary, they found that 'Carrick' meant rock – very appropriate, that made sense, nothing sinister about it.

'Noa – I wudn' advise that, Missus', was all that they could get out of the old fellow who lent them a hand one day of the week in the garden. For the rest, they were left to their own resources. They were 'furriners'. They came to feel that they were not particularly welcome – they sensed an atmosphere of suspicion, as if it rested on *them*, rather than on the place, for taking it on.

But why ever? *They* hadn't done anything. Were they regarded as intruders? Old inhabitants could easily convey that impression to newcomers invading sequestered coves cut off from the main tracks along the spine of the little land.

'Blue Waves' was indeed a totally un-Cornish house, quite out of keeping with its surroundings. For one thing it had a red-tiled roof like any suburban house up-country. For another, it was half a bungalow, most of it on the ground level, with a two-storey addition at the end, looking across to the detached garage. Inside, the chief feature was a good-sized hall, bedrooms and bathroom grouped around it – very convenient for a couple in their sixties. At the back a kitchen-living room, cosy wood-plank floor, and exceptionally large sink. All very well planned, the house had appeared as a model in a national newspaper in the 1920's, the model copied by a local builder.

What was wrong in giving the house a local name. Anything wrong in the name itself?

On this the gardener remained mum, as if there were.

English to the core, not suspicious like the Cornish or given to quirks of sensibility or precognition, in no way psychic, they innocently wondered if there were not something sinister in the 'howel' part of the name.

Anything to do with 'howl'? They could hear, as windy winter came on, a distinct howl at the back of the house, upon occasion — they thought, coming from the bluff.

The innocents were wrong in both suppositions. Someone acquainted with the old lost language might have supposed that it recorded an ancient Celtic personal name, Howel, familiar in Wales, and still a surname of a 'good' old family. Or, another possibility: could it refer to the 'huer' who in former days kept watch on the bluff to direct the fishermen as to the movements of the 'schools' (? shoals) of fish, once frequent in the bay? No longer.

The taciturn gardener did go so far as to tell them that the narrow path by their back wall did lead to the former huer's outpost on the bluff. But no more information.

Such silence, such reluctance to speak — like wringing blood out of a stone — aroused their curiosity, if not their suspicion. They began to watch, look out for little trails — above all, to listen.

*

That winter they felt certain that there were occasions when they heard a howl. It seemed to come from nearer than the bluff, they located it — or fancied they did — from the direction of the garage across the little court.

But could they pin it down to anything definite, to recognisable intervals? Gradually they thought that they could. It did not necessarily occur on windy days or nights, but always at the weekends. Eventually they thought that they could pin it down to Saturdays, and in the early evening, 'between the two lights', as the Cornish say.

A little later the wife heard a curious disturbing sound *within* the house — something between groan and stifled cry. And she heard it again. As with the louder howl from the garage, she determined to keep count. She noticed that the indoor sound was also heard only upon a Saturday, and that it followed upon the other within a matter of minutes — she could not be sure, perhaps ten, perhaps fifteen.

The curious thing about the indoor disturbance of the air, or atmosphere, vibration or whatever, was that her husband never once heard it. A practical fellow, of no imagination, he was ready to decry any thought of a cry, and to concentrate on getting the garden into shape, after a period of neglect.

All the same, was there a *something* about the house, some hoodoo upon it, that helped to account for the bargain they had acquired in the purchase price?

The garden indeed was in want of attention. Southward-looking combes in the West Country will turn into jungle in a humid summer, in a climate warm and wet and steamy.

The narrow strip between cliff and road was quite long, hidden from both by escallonia hedges, overgrown, of a rich and aromatic scent after rain, flowering blood-red. It took the newcomer and his old helper a fair time to get the upper garden in some order – fuchsias, veronicas, hydrangeas proliferated, in need of pruning and cutting back.

Deep down at the bottom was a waste space, trackless and almost impenetrable – nettles, brambles interlaced, ivy poisonously grappling the trees.

One day burrowing under what looked like a compost heap but was really a rubbish dump buried in leaves and ground ivy, the new owner came upon an old and damaged wheelbarrow, and not far away a lengthy crowbar. Wondering whether his handyman could repair the loose side of the wheelbarrow and make it still usable, he trundled his finds up the steep slope.

– To find his old helper transfixed by the spectacle, as if stunned; but it was the sight of the crowbar that loosened his tongue, frightened from suspicious silence into a torrent of gossip – a kind of release from an ugly spell. The story, pent up, rushed forth at length, but needed some intelligible order imposed upon it.

*

Gervase Bradninch was a not very successful solicitor in the little capital city of the county. He came from a really ancient family in the next county; they had come down in the world, and he had done nothing to rehabilitate their fortunes. This had made him a rather morose man and — with his reserve of pride, insisting on the county status of his family in the legal community in which he worked — did nothing to make him popular.

Nor did he work very hard. He had served in the first German war, 1914–18, risen to the rank of Major, and with his little clipped moustache, kept up his military bearing.

The best thing about him was his marriage — to a middle-class woman of no pretensions, much nicer than he was.

Nor was he any more successful with his family, a pleasant daughter who took after her mother, and a son who was a worse edition of himself.

The boy, hopefully named Guy after some remote Crusading ancestor, was indeed a peculiar child. He grew up into a handsome, masculine adolescent, with a precocious *penchant* for the girls, for all that he had been sent away to the old public school in Devon, to which generations of impecunious Bradninches had gone.

Bradninch and his wife made sacrifices to send him there — did their own housework, or rather Faith did, while he did the gardening. The sacrifice was ill rewarded: the youth made no progress.

The father did not improve matters by consistently discouraging the boy in whom he was so disappointed, regularly telling him that he was 'no good' at all, 'no good' at anything. Not even at games, though he was well built, and so not popular with his schoolmates. A sullen youth, he would never even try.

But he would try all right with the girls, and they as frequently responded. This was the one area of life in which he showed keenness, and he had what it takes to attract and give satisfaction in that small quarter.

They did not know how peculiar he was — that even as a boy he would stick a pen-knife into his thigh or leg, and swear that he felt nothing. Was this a brag? Or, if true, it indicated something to beware of, that needed attending to. And there were other odd signs.

The parents knew that the boy was odd, but — never having heard of Freud or Jung, the new psychology let alone Oedipus complex — accepted the situation, or accepted the perpetual irritation of it with a resigned sort of fatalism. Perhaps they hoped that one day it would just go away, resolve itself — it never crossed their minds that it might end fatally. Some responsive girl might take him on; the charity of women is inexhaustible — at any rate the instinct to perpetuate the race is. He would be quite good at *that*. And that would take him off their hands.

*

As a matter of fact, Oedipus complex did enter into the situation.

As the boy grew up into a fine show of puberty, exposing his well-equipped person on the beach below, sun bathing himself to a golden tan — for he was fair, like his remote Norman ancestors — on the rocks below, very convenient for assignations with their crevices and caves — his father came actively to dislike his good-for-nothing son. He did not know, or perhaps would not have cared if he had known, that his son nourished a perfect hatred pent up within him against his father.

Nothing Guy could do about it. His father held the purse-strings tight; anyway, nothing much in the purse to spare. The house on the coast, a dozen miles from the city, a daily drive to the office, had been something of an extravagance in the first place — and that had been regarded as put on for show: not residing like the other members of the legal confraternity in town where they made their living. Not much hobnobbing with the Bradninches. Had they any real friends?

The poor wife and mother did her best to keep peace between father and son, and there were no spontaneous outbreaks. Secretly, she sympathised with the handsome boy to whom she had given birth, rather shared his view of the father — as unsatisfactory as husband and father as Guy was as a son. Besides bullying his son all through adolescence, the father drank more than was good for him or his family. His wife had one or two women friends — not made welcome at 'Blue Waves' by her husband; so she confined herself to occasional exchanges at tea-time or elevenses, while Bradninch was away by day. Perhaps among their families there would be a girl who would yet make a man of her boy. She guessed, however, that he had a wider range of choice — was rather proud of that. It gave the poor woman more hope.

At last Guy chummed up with a more venturesome girl than usual, and, frustrated all along the line, at home as at school, developed a fixation for her, an obsession.

More trouble at home — he had no hope of a career, no prospects.

Obsessed with her as he was, was he really in love with her? Doubtful. He had plenty of sex, but no heart. That had been killed in him over the years — if it had ever existed. The girl, however, was game.

He proposed to her that they should make a run for it, and go off to London. He would drive — he was a demon driver. She was ready for the adventure, 'anything for fun,' she said, in their common lingo.

Where was the money to come from? She had none. O, Guy would see to that. He would pick her up at the cross-roads over the heave of hill, next Saturday evening, and they would make it through the night.

He drove like the fiend he was, up along A30, through Bodmin, through Okehampton, to Exeter and on.

Guy was pretty silent — nothing unusual about that, fine eyes intent on the road, an occasional flash from them. But he was, rather unusually, tense.

At length he said, 'Well, we have made a good get-away.'

She said, 'I wonder how our people will take it?'

He replied casually: 'No trouble with mine. I've killed them.'

He did not smile, but she took this as a joke, one of his occasional wild brags.

'What nonsense you talk, Guy dear.'

But it was not nonsense. He had.

He said nothing, but drove on faster than ever. It was not long past midnight when they reached London for their fun together.

*

Actually Guy had planned things, he thought, rather well. When his father got back from the office Guy was waiting for him in the garage, and caught him at the awkward moment of getting out of the car — with a crowbar. He was a powerful young man, and one blow was sufficient to crack his father's skull.

He made sure with another.

'Might as well finish the job,' he said and ran across the court, into the kitchen where his mother was bending over the sink washing vegetables for the evening meal. One blow from the crowbar, another to make sure, and she fell forward into the sink.

What next?

In the corner of the court was his father's big wheelbarrow (himself had never lent a hand with the gardening).

He shoved his father's still pulsating body clumsily into the wheelbarrow, and in the romantic twilight trundled it along the narrow path — knocking the head against the wall, what matter? Thence through the copse to the bluff, and threw the body over the edge to the rocks below, disturbing only the gulls.

A second journey disposed similarly of his mother's body. Small and light, she gave less trouble — more blood.

Thus busy, the problem resolved in his mind, he gave no thought to consequences — he never had done.

But — money for the planned week-end? He went back into the house, upstairs to his parents' bedroom, where they kept their cash. There wasn't much, so he rifled his mother's jewel-box for her few jewels.

It was all the work of an expeditious hour — never had he worked so well with a will.

He made his assignation at the crossroads and picked up his girl for the trip in his father's car, within a few minutes of seven.

*

It did not take long to get on the tracks or find the bodies, the wheelbarrow, the crowbar. Or to locate him and bring him to justice. After a brief trial he was, very properly, hanged.

Local opinion would have been outraged if he had not been. It was not only the crime in itself — and in those days people in a backward country district were not yet accustomed to murder, let alone murderers getting off a proper sentence.

It was the murder of father and mother that enraged the locality, and, in the odd way in which ordinary people get things out of proportion, they were even more set against him for taking his mother's jewels, and for such a purpose.

Of course, in our enlightened days a generation later, he would not have paid the penalty with his life. In those unphilosophic, illiberal days people said crudely, 'If you have a mad dog, you put him down.' Some added, 'better for the breed.'

In our more civilised days when there is so much less violence, people are more secure — particularly helpless old ladies with their purses and innocent young girls by the roadside glad of a lift in a car — and a benevolent society is at pains to maintain such mad dogs as an earlier, tougher society would have no compunction in putting down. And considered it a good riddance.

XI

The Will

The adolescent boy used to see the two sisters of an afternoon walking through the village from the school on the hill to their home in the town.

There was a great contrast in their appearance – one would hardly think they were sisters. The elder of the two was very dark, not particularly good-looking, but she was a personality. She was the Headmistress of the Infants' elementary school, and earned her own living – something exceptional for a country woman in those days before 1914. She walked with a slow, rather stately motion beneath long swaying skirts. She had a consciously precise way of speaking, very lady-like, twisting her mouth slightly to enunciate clearly and keep the ambitious youth in his place. She was very much in control.

Her sister was of much the same height, but totally different colouring. She had masses of ginger-gold hair, sexy coils of it, pale skin and prominent half-veiled blue eyes. It took the youth a little time to size up the situation and to realise that all was not quite right with her.

It was only occasionally that the younger, Stella, came up from town to meet her sister Margaret. Stella stayed at home all day, and did the housework, cooking and cleaning.

The growing boy noticed first that the elder always kept her sister away from him, on the inside of the pavement, while he accompanied them humbly, but briefly, in the gutter. Then he observed that he never got any talk with the younger – attempts on her part to put in a word were shouldered off, stifled even with an occasional 'Sh!'

He realised next, with something of a shock, that what the younger said was nonsense, *décousue*, not sewn up – he was rather good at French at his grammar school.

'I suppose you feel very superior to us now,' said his former Headmistress, who had known him as a boy — keeping him too in his place with her curious twist of mouth.

'Big boy, big boy,' came from the inside pavement.

'Yes, you're a big fellow for your age,' the elder said hurriedly to end the subject.

'Big enough to be married. Big—' he thought he heard something unsuitable (he was a youthful prig, and didn't like such plain speaking).

'Sh!', came from the elder, who ended the talk with practised skill, hustling him off he hardly knew how. But in going he caught an unmistakable leer in the sad, grey-blue eyes; and, though he had not much sense and did not care for women, he knew what *that* look meant.

*

The fact was that both women were distinctly sexy, not only the younger one. The village on the hill knew that Margaret — always deferentially referred to as Miss Tregenza — was the 'favourite' of the Headmaster of the Senior School next door, if not precisely his 'fancy woman', as they called it.

He was a rather low-slung fellow, with a curious shuffling gait — he wore spats — and was already balding: said by those who know to be an indication of potency. There were other indications too, to those who used their eyes. For one thing he had a large, fleshy proboscis of a nose, and, often enough, a hand in his pocket to quell the ready reaction at the nubile girls passing before him. Instinct told *them* what was what, and where it came in.

Everybody knew that he was married to a sourpuss of a wife twenty years older than himself. The village knew too that when school was over, and the coast clear, he often crossed the school-yard the back way to pay a visit to his colleague. Nothing came of it — at any rate, nothing awkward, that might be visible. The Headmistress was a dab at keeping awkward things under control — witness her sister.

'What has she got that I haven't got?' said an envious (female) colleague.

'Breasts — a full bosom,' Headmaster could have replied.

Both sisters had those ample amenities.

Margaret had her fun, cagily, unacknowledged — nobody could, or dared, bring it up against her. Stella had none — and yet she was a far more desirable piece, physically, if it had not been that the menfolk knew she was queer in the head. She was odd, not mad — what the local people called in their lingo, 'not 'zackly'.

Their father, a widower, was the manager of the Weighbridge in the town. As the town's trade prospered, so did he. He weighed in the heavy stuff, chiefly coal and lime, but also early vegetables from the Islands, that came up the little one-track railway from the neighbouring port.

He was concerned about his younger daughter. The town unkindly said that he had quite a tidy sum on offer to the fellow who would take her on and marry her. There were no offers.

Margaret had all the luck. The Headmaster's prematurely ageing wife, with complaining down-turned mouth — she had plenty to complain about — died. He was able to marry his fancy and, before it was too late — she was already in her forties — give her a baby-daughter.

*

Years passed.

The schoolboy, grown up, had a career away from home, but kept in touch with events there.

At some point — he did not know precisely when — the Headmaster died. He was years older than Margaret. Both she and he had pensions; their growing daughter was well provided for.

The Weighbridge master was even better off; when he died he left a handsome provision for his otherwise unprovided younger daughter.

The two sisters lived comfortably together — now perhaps in their early sixties — with the growing girl, Margaret's daughter, Stella's niece. Everything would come to her. She should be marriageable enough, and marry very well, when her time came.

As time went on the household became less comfortable.

Stella got queerer and more eccentric — never downright
looney, sufficient to 'send her to Bodmin', as the phrase went:
which meant the County Lunatic Asylum (now, in contemporary jargon, Mental Hospital).

All her life Margaret had had this 'millstone round her neck',
as she put it to herself; she had done her duty — and more, she
felt — by her sister.

As Stella got older she became more of a trial; she relapsed
into something like childhood. Her habits got odder: she would
go up to a looking-glass, offer herself chocolate, and get quite
angry when it was not taken. She was also rather sluttish, no
help in the house, much more of a liability.

With no unkindness in her heart, Margaret grew weary of her
antics and the unending job of keeping an eye on her.

At last she saw an advertisement of a suitable establishment
in a nearby town, in which to place her. A private home offered
a room for an elderly person, lady or gentleman, who would be
properly cared for by the owner, a qualified nurse — Margaret
knew the name as a respectable one.

Conscientiously she went to inquire and inspect. The
matronly owner said candidly that her preference was for a
gentleman — less trouble. However, she didn't mind, and was
ready to take Stella for a little extra to take extra trouble with
her. Stella was now rather feeble; Margaret did not want her to
fall downstairs or out of the window.

The ladies agreed on a pound a week extra. Margaret made it
clear that money was no object, her sister being quite well off.
They parted amicably, and Margaret was seen off at the gate by
a large shambling fellow, of indeterminate age, whom she could
not quite place — perhaps a gardener or handyman: the Home
needed such a fellow, evidently a working-man.

The sister was happily placed, all with her agreement —
something new in her life at last: she was well contented and
very well looked after. The Home was fairly near, and Margaret
went over every week to see how Stella was getting on.

Two or three months thus passed.

Then came a week when Margaret was told that her sister was
not very well and didn't want to see anybody.

The same thing the next week.

The third week she rang up, and the information was still the same.

The fourth week she was called away on a business engagement concerning her father's estate, and came back herself unwell.

Thus four or five weeks passed, and she grew suspicious — she must *see* her sister at any rate, one read such dreadful things in the papers nowadays.

She rang up to make sure and fix an appointment. She was told that her sister was now perfectly well and would be delighted to see her — had been hoping to see her indeed the week before.

She went over. Her sister came down from her room — perfectly well and contented, even more so than before, a faint glow of pleasure in the faded cheeks, dull old eyes a bit brighter.

They chatted away about their health — Margaret had had flu — nothing wrong with Stella that she recalled; no inquiry after her niece — nothing odd in that, she was so forgetful (*décousue* had been the word years ago).

Then the Home's owner, very qualified matron, came in.

'Have you told your sister your news?'

'No.'

'Oh, you must tell her, you know.'

A blush rose on the pale cheeks, she hung her head like a child. No reply — a sudden shyness overcame her. But it was evidently of a pleasurable character.

Going out into the lobby, the matron said, in matronly-wise:

'Her news she wouldn't tell you — she has married my son.'

This was the large docile animal, of about twenty-five, useful about the place, whom Margaret had had a glimpse of at the gate.

And, of course, all arrangements about the will had to be altered in consequence.

XII

The Doctor's Family

Miss Millicent was always known as 'Miss Millie' without any surname, so well was the name of her father, the small town's prime surgeon, known in it. Indeed, he too did not need his surname: to everybody he was 'the Doctor', *tout court* — 'the Doctor's fields', 'the Doctor's stables'. He was proud of his carriage and horses, and usually paid an early morning visit to the courtyard behind his house in High Cross Street (the cross had long vanished, beyond the time of which anyone had any remembrance), before setting out on his rounds.

'See, see, see, Rawe' — his mannerisms were rather like George III's, repetitive and inconsequent — he would say to his favourite groom, giving him instructions for the day. 'See, see. What?'

Those were the days when the Doctor was still active, and occupied the three-storeyed granite house with the steps down into the street, iron railings long since vanished to make way for the increase of traffic the growing china-clay industry provided. In the great blizzard of 1891, when the West Country was covered in snow all through March and April, and trains were actually snowed in on Dartmoor, the snow came right up over the steps against the front door.

The Doctor had done very well in life — and looked it: a large man, fat and tight as a beer-barrel about the waist, frock-coated and top-hatted, purple complexion like the port in his cellar. Contentedly married, two children only, one of each sex — everything seemed well arranged and all set fair.

But was it?

Some doubt arose about his young hopeful of a son approaching manhood. He had not been much good at school — nothing odd about that. But his tastes were unaccountably low. Instead of making his companions among those of his own class — few enough, but there were the families of the local lawyer, the steward of the Duchy estates in the neighbourhood, even the Rector (with eligible daughters all too available), young Dick preferred the stable companions, in particular his father's groom.

There had been a *contretemps* between Doctor and Rector. A load of manure being carted from the stables uphill to 'Doctor's fields' had had the mischance to upset just outside the Rectory — and, of all things, on a Sunday, when the Rector was issuing forth for church. He preached his sermon on the ungodly proceeding of Sunday labour, aimed recognisably at the Doctor, sitting stiff and red-faced in his pew. With the consequence that he ceased attending church thenceforward.

It was many years later that the local historian saw the old Doctor, blubber-faced, tears rolling unashamedly down the bloated cheeks, at the graveside of his former critic — not long before he was to roll into his own grave.

*

All was indeed not well with the Doctor's son and heir, for whom he pitched his expectations too high. Or was it so unreasonable to expect young Richard to succeed to the busy practice the Doctor had built up?

'Doctor' was an impatient, irritable man, and his favourite terms for the youth were 'Slowcoach, Duffer, Good-for-nothing. See, see, see.'

'No good at school: no interest in the surgery — his only interest skulking all day about the stables with the men.'

'You must be patient with him, Richard,' said his much-tried spouse; the son had been called after his father. 'Remember he is my boy.'

'He is, indeed. Not much of me in him that I can see.'

No reply could be made to that, for the Doctor was convinced that his wife — with whom he lived agreeably enough, since she subjected herself to his every whim — had imported a strain of weakness into the stock. She, son Richard and daughter Millicent were all 'easy-going' as the household put it with polite meiosis.

However, the Doctor was bent on young Richard being trained for his own profession — for which he had no aptitude and which, secretly, he hated. The young man was entered at the London hospital where the Doctor had done his own training.

It was not long before he came back, a 'returned empty'. Worse than that was the conclusion in the back-yard among the stablemen. The sight of the knife and the smell of blood, they put it crudely, had 'turned his mind' (small blame to him).

The Doctor, obstinate as usual, would not accept the state of the case in this instance, it touched his pride too nearly. And young Richard, returning home, skulked about the place much as before. Except that there was a new arrival in the household to awaken his interest.

This was a handsome young female, three or four years older than himself, who had been recruited as part-housemaid, part-companion for Miss Millicent — at any rate, she shared her bed at night-time.

For Miss Millie was subject to night terrors. As a girl she had always had a nurse. Now adolescent, approaching womanhood, she could not face the ordeal of a bedroom by herself, at least at night-time.

The Doctor, who had a remedy for everything — except his sullen, refractory son — readily solved this problem.

He had been called in to an interesting *accouchement*. A girl of a respectable family he knew on a neighbouring estate had been seduced by a bright young spark of the family — which accepted responsibility and arranged for the child to be adopted by its grandmother, in the usual way in such cases, as if its mother, the last offspring in the long tale of her progeny.

The young woman was of rather superior character and more than common pride, deeply wounded by what had befallen her. She was available: here was a solution to her problem. She became Miss Millie's companion by night, if not by day; for the rest, a reliable housemaid, suitably trained in grander establishments than the Doctor's.

One possibility, one contingent source of danger, had not occurred to his practical, unimaginative mind. The new recruit was a remarkably handsome young woman, and it was not long before the Doctor's son fell for her.

She did not encourage him, her own shattering experience was too recent for that. But, by the same token, she could not help a consoling word when she ran into him about the house, or in the back-yard. Young Richard made occasion to run into her whenever he could: he sensed her sympathy — two wounded souls. He knew her story, of course, and that his 'easy-going' sister doted on her.

No one knew the depth of his own inner torment, until the fact spoke out loud — too loud for everybody's happiness.

*

Her son's fixation was not long in discovering itself to his mother: the Doctor, of course, had noticed nothing.

When apprised of the state of the case, he took a step well worthy of his practical sagacity. Knowing the girl's family — 'he knew too much,' she said — he made interest with her mother to get her married — well, married off. Rather more than 'nothing loth', the mother wanted nothing better than to see her daughter safely married. But to whom?

This presented no problem to the Doctor: there was his favourite groom, Rawe. Hopelessly enamoured of Miss Millie's night-companion — as the Doctor's wife well knew — Rawe thought of nothing better than having this handsome piece, if of 'damaged goods', as they put it in the stable-yard, for his own.

What of the girl?

She was not the least in love with the groom — had in fact fancied something higher for herself in submitting to her lover's embraces, the Squire's younger son. With her bitter experience, a vein of iron was to show itself in her life: no illusions. 'Beggars can't be choosers,' her motto; her motive, 'to cover up me shaame.'

The wedding took place, the regulation silver teapot presented by the Doctor and his wife; a modest little cottage found for the happy couple up in the village, just below 'Doctor's fields' where the groom could as conveniently look after his horses and cattle.

A 'happy couple'?

Rawe, a simple, kindly soul, adored the wife he had not expected to achieve — 'worshipped the ground she trod on', according to one observer.

Her attitude? No one knew. She put up a brave face to the world, cared nothing for the village life, encouraged no confidences. As the world went, they made a respectable couple, and kept to themselves, few friends.

*

A much grander *accouchement* the Doctor was called in for: the wife of the Lord Lieutenant, at their romantic castle in its cove by the sea, was expecting her first child. Great was the fuss and preparation. The Doctor, leaving an assistant to look after his surgery, was expected to stay at the Castle until the delivery. His wife bustled about to pack his dress-clothes, stiff shirt, gold cuff-links called into display.

It was the bluebell time of the year. The Doctor's fields were rampant with bluebells, the air filled with the sound of distant churchbells coming over the hillside on the Sunday when the Doctor was called away, that his son found a convenient corner by the cattle-trough, and shot himself.

*

Not long after this the Doctor — no son to succeed him — sold his practice and retired. He had done very well financially, one of the early birds to get in on the ground in investing profitably in the district's expanding china-clay industry.

He bought himself a grander house than the somewhat cramped premises, with the dispensary in which he had made up his coloured waters for the credulous simpletons who badgered him for them — the more disagreeable the taste, the better they felt for it. (The favourite groom was a constant addict, fool that he was.)

The Doctor's new house was in the oddly named Palace Road. No one knew why its name, though true it was that the nobs of the town had their villa residences there — mostly stone-built, grey granite, stepped gables and turrets, though the grandest of all was a palatial villa in smooth cream colour-wash.

The old couple did not long survive retirement, leaving their ample fortune to Miss Millicent, still unmarried.

Who was there to take care of her?

Her banker.

He was an unmarried Scot, and the *amitié amoureuse* continued for years. Everybody said that he was after her money — so why didn't he marry her?

Everybody said, in the usual way, that they lived together. Oddly enough, everybody was wrong. Perhaps neither of them was a marrying sort. What he did for her was to look after her money for her — and, my goodness, how it mounted up!

When she died, in middle age, she left it all to him. So everybody said, 'There you are — you see. We always said he'd get it all.'

But, when he died, not many years after her, he surprised everybody by leaving the whole fortune to the local hospital.

He made one provision — for a stained-glass window in memory of them in our church. So there they are, the whole family rounded up in glass.

XIII

The Collaborator

As a famous novelist he had long ago built up effective defences
against the menace of women. He had always fancied a career
for himself and had no intention of subordinating his to them,
or even sharing it, let alone subjugating himself to the purposes
of Nature and perpetuating the race. As for that, he agreed
with Villiers de l'Isle Adam, it could be left to the servants.

When barely beginning to be known he had been pestered by
the letters of one Jacintha Lillicrap — appalling name — who
sent him specimens of her Old Gothic script, Beowulf in the
original, along with little perfumed albumy booklets for him to
write in. He intuited that she was a poor girl. He did not respond
to her plea for a meeting — he remembered Montherlant's
provincial blue-stocking, who got caught in the revolving door
of the restaurant to which he took her to lunch.

An upper-class girl, with whom he became friendly, said,
'Don't I know that there is a glass screen let down all round you,
on which I bark my shins and cannot get through?' A woman of
equal birth, but of less sense, tried to break through the barrier
and force herself upon his carefully preserved intimacy. She
would — unasked-for — knit him socks, ring him up to ask for his
cat to whom he *was* devoted (she, the cat, made no demands)
and he hated being telephoned. Once, when they met, she said:

'O yes, I'm coming to Trevarrick all right.' This was the
distinguished old house in a Cornish combe, a cosy little estate,
which he had won for himself with his hard-earned earnings.

Little did she know that such female confidence shocked him.
She was never allowed to penetrate the solitude of Trevarrick.

A wartime widow of a gallant gun-boat officer fell for a
volume of autobiography the novelist wrote: she fancied a
remarkable resemblance between her husband and the writer

(no idea how wrong she was). She wrote him reams and reams of her own autobiography, twenty-page letters he had not time to read, let alone inclination. He did not reply. That did not discourage her.

He took to sending them back unread — eventually recognising her hand, unopened. (He could not *bear* them.) Still not quite discouraged, she planned to meet him at a lunch with mutual friends, which she found he had accepted. He discovered the trick, and cried off going.

She never succeeded in meeting him.

*

The case was different with his French translator, a distinguished woman in her own right, bilingual, for she was French on her father's side, English on her mother's. Or rather, Cornish on one side, Breton on the other — so, a pure Celt, with all the advantages of the Celtic temperament (and some of the disadvantages): more than her fair share of feminine perception and intuition, and similarly of female *personalism*, taking everything in a personal sense, subjectively. No masculine objectivity — but how could that be expected? All the same it irritated him.

He had been able to defend himself the more easily because, all through the first half of his career, he was almost entirely homosexual in his interests. Thoroughly acquainted with him through his work, as she was, this she had come to accept. At times, a pang of jealousy, but no reproach — too much sense for that. A clever woman, she was acquainted with that inflexion in her own family.

Arriving at middle age he felt a stirring of interest in the opposite sex. Was he undergoing a change? Earlier, bent on fulfilling himself in his work, an absorbed egoist, he had rigidly repressed any such leanings. Now, more fulfilled, having acquired something like fame and fortune, he felt safe, and consequently more responsive — at any rate, more ready to respond. Perhaps less unready.

Madeleine, his translator, the closest scrutiniser of his text, noticed the signs in his work, and was not without hope of him.

In a sense, more than anyone, she had grown along with him, developed alongside of him, though at a distance — across the Channel at its widest. She owed much to him — as he did to her.

Did she realise, clever woman that she was, that *au fond* his need of her was greater, for it related to his work? There was the male egoism: he needed her for his work, he was dependent on her for translating it, rather than it was her he needed.

This element in the situation remained unexplained between them, unexplored. Perhaps it was as well.

*

A bigger book than usual, a longer stint of translation, required some consultation and putting of heads together. A meeting seemed more convenient, and Julian invited Madeleine over — or, in his own view, consented to a visit, to tidy things up and put the book in order for the press.

She at any rate penetrated Trevarrick, if no further. It was a country mansion of some size, with a long westward wing. She found herself comfortably provided in the wing — her own study, bedroom and bathroom — housekeeper's apartment securely between wing and front of the house where Julian 'kept' (the old term he held to from Cambridge days).

Work over, he accompanied her politely up to the Plymouth-Roscoff ferry, and saw her safely off on her journey across Channel.

Back came a letter of the kind he did not like to receive. Along with thanks for his kind care of her (no particular care of her, he reacted, nothing out of the way, just common hospitality), she had remained on board to watch his retreating figure along the quay, 'with mingled desperation and hope'.

What had that to do with him? he reflected testily. Hope of what? And why 'desperation'?

Their relations were on a perfectly good footing, profitable to both. She was necessary to his work — he appreciated that. He confided everything about his work to her, he had trust in her literary advice and valued it as well as her linguistic expertise. Since his work mattered to him more than anything, he put the

best of himself into his letters to her. Couldn't she be content
with that?

This she knew, and treasured his letters in consequence. She
kept them carefully in file, docketed and annotated with her
comments and notes for reply, they ranged over years and
constituted an indispensable source for his biography.

Well-aware of his egoism — the vocational disease of writers
— she knew that he valued his side of the correspondence more
than anything.

He decided not to take up the personal point offered for
discussion, but to confine himself to their present literary
project. This he went into fully, final settlement of points
agreed, plans for future work, etc. He closed the gap with a
generous cheque for her expenses.

*

Work proceeded on both sides of the Channel. Next year a
meeting was necessary to settle points at issue on his next book —
a translation of a biography he much admired (his French,
adequate enough, was much less good than her idiomatic
English).

He suggested as *venue* Mont St Michel, which he wanted to
compare with his own familiar St Michael's Mount.

He found himself rather disappointed with the greater, more
historic monument. Of course, there was no comparison archi-
tecturally between the magnificent Romanesque and early
Gothic abbey, and the little Cornish church on top of its Mount.
But the very smallness of the latter made it integral, one with
the Rock — 'the Grey Rock in the Wood' as its old Cornish name
described it; whereas the very mass of the buildings imposed on
Mont St Michel seemed to him out of proportion and to dwarf
the natural site.

*

Some months later, when the next piece of collaboration had
been completed, he got a letter resurrecting a phrase that had
cropped up in the course of their joint work, to which she
attached what he considered unwarranted significance.

'Memory and Desire, your phrase,' [she wrote] 'how that expresses my feeling as to our relations. I have indeed had little other to go on over the years than Memory — memories of our all too brief meetings, encounters rather, and with what Desire I have looked forward to them, little enough to feed on in the long intervals between one and the other of them. All too few, when life runs through our fingers like snow melting, or sand in an hour-glass. Isn't there an English poet who writes of "the sands of Time"?'

He couldn't remember, and he couldn't be bothered to look it up. After all, she was his research-assistant, not he hers. Nor did he like the tone of intimacy, the suggestion of it the message conveyed.

However, he had a residual kindness of heart, a not unwilling sympathy of mind, and replied how much pleasure the visit to her native soil had given him — *la douce France, mère des arts, des armes, et des lois*, and the rest of it — and how much he had enjoyed their conversations.

At the next round in their work and their relations this move-forward on his part produced the suggestion of another visit, since she was coming across the Channel to see friends. Might she come down to the West Country for a week-end at the end of her stay?

At this he took evasive action: he had to be away from home over that week lecturing at a neighbouring university. The excuse was plausible enough, but seen through.

Kindness came breaking in, and some months later he agreed to meet her when passing through Paris on his way to the Riviera.

This was followed by further pressure, more insistent invasion of his privacy.

She was well aware of the existence of his 'nephew', Mark — sometimes Julian referred to him as his 'adopted son' — and that this was the real love of his life. She could not understand it, but she had the sense to appear to accept it, even to pretend to regard it with sympathy. After all, it did not compete with the love of a woman — there was no woman in Julian's life: a mere boy was no rival.

All the same, though expressing the sentiment, hoping to win a sign of regard for its nobility, if not renunciation, she could not refrain from voicing her woman's confidence, a suggestion of reproach. In inquiring kindly after Mark — away doing his military training — she hoped he was doing well. Yet, 'what could a boy give him that a mature woman could not give? — greater understanding, depth of sympathy', etc, all that.

Julian knew that line well. Had he not encountered it years before, with an American woman friend:

'I wish I knew a way to seduce you.' On that occasion he had merely smiled to himself with the thought: 'The only way would be if you were a handsome boy.'

However, he deeply appreciated Madeleine's efforts on behalf of his *work*, and realised that it was largely owing to them that it was recognised in France, a greater source of satisfaction to him than any belated recognition in his own country.

She thought of her work for him as in the nature of a collaboration — as if she were his wife. And at last it was rewarded by his promotion to Commander of the Legion of Honour.

He went over to Paris to receive it — a day of triumph for her, who thought in such terms, even more than for him, who did not.

Her triumph released the springs of her emotions more unguardedly than before: welcome to him or no, she made no doubt of her love for him over the years.

'Did you notice that I kissed the *bouton* of your *légion d'honneur*, rather than saluting you with a kiss on your cheeks, let alone on your lips, so prim and expressive of your reserve? I regard my gesture of recognition as a symbol of my whole attitude — also, in its way, controlled, making no demands on you. Surely you realise that? Then I can read the whole spectrum of expressions on your face over the years, and know them all so well. — Only one missing, and that is the deepest *chagrin* of my life.'

Que faire? was his reaction to this declaration. He was more than irritated — vexed by it. It was taking the pattern of those earlier experiences, from more abrupt, less subtle and sensitive souls. But now — in middle age! — he saw a ridiculous side to the situation. And, ever suspicious, hadn't there been a Freudian suggestion in her kissing his *bouton*?

In a kind of liturgical antiphony, conducted on his side within his own mind, he reacted impatiently: 'She can kiss my arse.'

This was not the kind of thing to say out loud, for he was dependent on her. With the doubled selfishness of both man and writer, he would continue to make use of her — her services were indispensable, and these he appreciated. He rewarded them generously enough — financially. He was not mean about money, unlike his chief rival as novelist, promoted to the *Académie française*, making a fool of himself with specially tailed green uniform, sword and all. (But *he* was more generous in his contacts with women, always ready to give himself, or what he had, rather than cash.)

Now:

'I *believe* that you like me to love you. And, *mon cher*, you shall be indulged. — Even at the risk of irritating you. For you must realise quite well that I cannot help myself. And I always excuse myself for that by saying, That is the way I am made: if he doesn't like it, *tant pis*.'

Oddly enough for a man, he was subtler than she was. She was a woman, all of one piece. As a homosexual, he had a great deal of feminine intuition. As a Celt, he considered himself psychic — and was. Once she had said: 'You have an unfair advantage, with your double dose of intuition, feminine as well as masculine.'

This had been some years before — an earlier flare-up about Mark, when she had urged that she had far greater understanding of him than a mere boy.

A masculine sense of justice — a disadvantage in his dialogue with her, now forced by her into the open — led him to admit

that this was true enough. She *did* understand him better than
Mark — but that was precisely what he wanted to avoid.

And why should she want to bring things — better unexpressed,
or hinted at — into the open? Couldn't she be contented with his
friendship, sincere enough, enduring enough over years, for all
that it was rooted in his need of her and her use to him?

At last, contrary to the rule he set himself in such *affaires du
cœur*, he came clean in a crisp sentence, not brutally, but
making his own reaction to it clear.

'Yes, this is why sometimes I do not feel at ease in your company. Friendship — yes, with all my heart. You say that you
are as you are and cannot help yourself. May this not also be
true for me? We are as we are, as we are made, and cannot be
other. My gospel, my rule of life, is to follow my own nature.'

He realised, as he wrote, that this was true for her too. So their
natures were in direct confrontation now, their relations stuck,
static, no further movement possible.

To this came an open appeal: 'Can you not save me from the
ultimate bitterness that all my efforts have been utterly unproductive of any good to you or me?'

This made him angry. He realised again — though this was
weakness on his part — that there was justice in the reproach.
But this was emotional blackmail, and he would not submit to
it. Wasn't deep and lasting friendship enough? Moreover, with
masculine objectivity, he rejected the feminine subjectivity of
the argument that all her efforts — *their* efforts, he emended —
had been 'utterly unproductive of any good to you or me'.

Typical feminine exaggeration, he replied silently, anti-
phonally; also quite untrue. Hadn't their joint efforts been
quite exceptionally rewarding, to both him and her? For him, a
public in France; for her, a continuous occupation, something
of a literary career.

For himself he reflected that, if only she would let up this
emotional pressure, for ever demanding what he could not give,
he could be perfectly natural with her.

In fact, he had great natural charm — one of the chief sources of attraction to women — that went with the ambivalence of his nature. But he could never afford to be his natural self with her. He had always to be on guard. And this, he decided, was just a Bore. (He had regulated his life precisely to avoid being *bored* by humans, in any way.)

This something-of-a-showdown produced a slightly decipherable change in her attitude — for the good, he considered: one of acceptance? Perhaps.

She thought up excuses for him. (Privately, he thought this impertinent, but decided to take no notice.) She put forward the view that he had been defeated in the struggle with the sensual side of his nature. That he had needed to prove to himself that it was not through weakness that he could conquer his affections. Thus he had inhibited them, until he had smothered them.

This made him laugh, a little wryly: pure feminine self-delusion. He had not smothered his affection for, devotion to, Mark. He saw through her argument for what it was — an excuse to save her own pride, the rejection of her proffered love, over years.

Like so many women, she nursed herself with a fantasy: what *she* could have been to him, if only he had not preferred Mark. She had forced herself, in appearance at any rate, to accept that fact. Pride forbade her to accept a mere boy — now grown into a handsome young man of independent talent — as a rival.

She was due for a revelation. For a change occurred in Julian's life too — a far more decisive, a more creative one than any shifting of the cards she held in her hand.

*

Madeleine had a niece, a clever girl student of English literature at the Sorbonne, immensely *enthousiasmée* with the work of her aunt's famous friend, and all agog to meet him. She besought her aunt to arrange a meeting on his next visit to Paris. It would be an interview, encouragement for her work — she was intending a career as a journalist.

Willing to help, Madeleine had no misgivings.

Oddly enough, Julian had. However, the interview was arranged.

Julian entered on it with some misgivings — another chore. Still, Madeleine wished it, and — since he could not oblige her in the great thing that mattered most to her — the more reason to oblige her in small things.

It turned out no laughing matter at all.

Ominously he remembered what had been said to him as a young man at the university, by a remarkable Levantine Jewess, married to a brilliant but unresponsive authority on Greek vases. (He too preferred the young athletes depicted on them.)

She had said, 'It would need a young Greek girl to penetrate your defences.'

In Madeleine's niece he was at length confronted by the prophesied Greek girl.

Not that she was Greek, or at all dark. She was, unlike her aunt, very fair, pale cream-coloured skin, close-cropped flaxen-gold hair, intent eyes of a magnetic blue-green. She looked like a beautiful boy, and — with all the freedom of her generation — a whole generation younger than Madeleine and Julian, half their age — made no bones about setting out to seduce him.

The interview was followed by other meetings. The girl had all the persistence of her aunt, with twice her attractiveness, an unconsidered boyish charm.

Everything about Madeleine was calculation — an element in her make-up that put off her intended captive.

What Julian had not reckoned on in one so young was that a similar element was present in the niece: she was on edge with desire to produce a child by the famous writer.

'Well, why not take a risk?' thought Julian; he was well provided for any consequences.

Of course, she had her way, and proved pregnant.

*

Madeleine was by way of writing in her new mood, of acceptance of the situation between Julian and her, how much she appreciated '*les petits soins*' he took with her — little gestures like carrying her coat, lighting her cigarette, paying for a meal they took together, the very tone of voice with which he told her he liked her dress.

Little did she guess that he regarded '*les petits soins*' one had to take when women were about as yet another bore. And as for lighting her cigarette — well, he detested smoking.

The fact of her niece's pregnancy was not withheld from Madeleine, nor the steps taken for looking after her. Madeleine was enraged — and not for her niece. She was enraged at them both.

Writing him a last letter, she exploded with anger: the sight of the pregnant girl, she wrote, made her physically sick. 'Keep your barriers,' she said, 'you know that I have never tried to get through them or round them.'

Subjectivism — self-delusion, he registered; hadn't this been just what she had been trying to do through all the years he had known her?

Passionate love converts easily enough into passionate hatred. 'When I think what she is carrying in her womb, and *whose offspring* it is, I hate you both.'

No sympathy for the niece, no regard for the future.

With the absolutism of her temperament all relations were broken off.

For himself, he would have to find another translator, in place of her who had served him so well.

He was not unprepared for this. Once more, the doubled egoism of man and writer gave him to think — hadn't he a replacement in the clever niece? Couldn't he train her to take her aunt's place — with the advantage that her work would appeal more to her younger generation, a positive gain?

He had reckoned without Madeleine. She, whom life-long love had taught to know him better than anyone, knew his most vulnerable point, what he cared for more than anything, the egoism involved with his writing.

She possessed the long correspondence that threw most light, year after year, upon his work: invaluable for its interpretation, indispensable, to any future biography.

Carefully, with the conscientiousness with which she had

preserved them all those years, but with grim determination she abstracted all his letters from her files, took them down into the backyard and burned them in the common incinerator.

XIV

The End of the Trewinnards

The word 'winnard' is still alive in Cornish dialect. My mother would say, 'You'm cold as a dyin' winnard'; or there used to be the phrase 'blue as a winnard'. Outside of blowy Newquay a place at an exposed cross-roads is called 'Winnard's Perch'. I think that the bird in question would be a plover, inhabitant of the uplands.

Though Trewinnard in the parish of St Erth, near St Ives, is not upland country, it lies near it, and in olden days would be a haunt of plover, since it was then mostly open downs and marshes.

Trewinnard itself − place of that bird − occupied a good patch of cultivable land in the midst of all that. Hence the settlement, and the older Tudor house − subsequently transformed into the fine, silvery granite house of the late 17th century, Queen Anne and all that, with ancient bowling green for the delectation of the family, cosily beside it.

This may not be as ancient as the family, a medieval one, which had come to an end there before the end of the 17th century.

The apogee of the family, or at least the moment when they entered the page of history, briefly, was the reign of Henry VIII. Indeed, with that they reach the law-books, the text-books of constitutional history, with the test case of John Trewinnard, Member of Parliament for St Ives.

He was heavily encumbered by debts; but the point of being a member of Parliament then was that it gave one the privilege of not being sued for debt while Parliament was sitting. During the intervals between sessions of the long Reformation Parliament, Trewinnard stood on guard within his premises, keeping creditors at bay.

One day the biggest of these, to whom he was most heavily in debt, obtained a writ of outlawry against him. On the strength of this, he broke Trewinnard's defences, entered the house by force, and carried him off to ward under the sheriff's jurisdiction, until the next session of Parliament.

Trewinnard thereupon brought suit of *habeas corpus* against his creditor, in the expectation of large damages for unlawful imprisonment of a MP. (These would handsomely offset his debt.)

The point at issue was — how far did his protection as MP run? Did it extend to intervals between sessions, when he was no longer attending Parliament?

The House of Commons itself heard his suit. It decided that Trewinnard *as an outlaw* could not claim the King's protection, and therefore could not sit as MP until he had compounded with his creditor. Trewinnard was compelled to sue out the King's pardon of his outlawry, and upon that was enabled to take his seat in Parliament as before.

Trewinnard had a son, who held a good office under the Duchy of Cornwall as Steward of the Stannaries, i.e. the courts regulating the tin mining from which a considerable proportion of the Duchy's revenues arose (surplus-value, in Marxist terminology, which supported the heir to the Crown through the ages).

This Trewinnard had a son, who belied his name of Deiphobus, by killing a man in an access of rage and folly. He buried the body secretly in the chapel at Trewinnard. (Does his ghost haunt the house?)

Not so secretly but that the coroners came to hear of it. They searched house and chapel, opened the grave and found the body. A jury sat and returned the undoubted fact. Conducted to a neighbouring Justice of the Peace, his *mittimus* was made out and he was taken up to Launceston gaol to await Assizes.

There he languished for some months in the insalubrious confinement of the dungeon known as Doomsdale, by the postern gate — all so graphically described by the Quaker, George Fox, in his *Journal* in the next century.

The unfortunate Trewinnard had a friend — fortunately for him — in Sir Reginald Mohun, who had some pull at Court.

Deiphobus applied to him for help in his desperate plight — no doubt of his guilt, or of the death penalty for murder in those more realistic days.

The powerful Sir Reginald and his client Deiphobus reached an understanding. Trewinnard would plead manslaughter, acting in self-defence. Mohun would pull the necessary strings at Court to obtain pardon, and assure him life.

Naturally a heavy consideration would pass for so handsome a favour — no less than the making over to Mohun of the ancient estate which the Trewinnards had held from time immemorial.

Came the Assizes at Launceston: the jury found Trewinnard guilty, and he was condemned to death. Thereupon Sir Reginald placed the condemned man's reprieve in the hands of the Sheriff, and execution was stayed.

Sureties, however, were taken, and given, for Trewinnard's future conduct, whereupon he was released.

He lived out his days quietly enough — nothing more is recorded of him — upon a small allowance made to him out of the lands that had once been his and given his ancient family its name.

XV

The House at the Cross-Roads

There it is in the mind's eye, as it was at any time in the hundred and more years of its existence: now made a clean sweep of for road-widening. Its curious shape had been dictated by the roads: in the front bending back like the side of an old-fashioned heating iron, clipped inward at either end, on one side by the lane, on the other by the approach to the carpenter's shop and the village smithy. What it was like at the back was not to be deciphered. An irregular tetrahedron, built in the gaunt granite of the district, streaked with copper, it always had a forbidding appearance before even the sinister story that came to be enacted within it filled it with horror.

It had been two cottages, one room up and one down, originally. Then, back in the last century, one of them had been inhabited by a middle-aged woman and her daughter. The woman was unmarried; not even the village, which knows everything, knew who the father was. Such was the strength of character of mother and growing daughter that they were treated with marked respect. We were not clear how they kept body and soul together, for Miss Angwin did not 'go out to work' like other women in the village. She kept a small sweet-shop: that must have been when the second cottage was annexed to the first and a door made through the wall up and down.

Poverty was extreme; but pride was almost equal. It was the poverty that engendered so many of the stories of those days, that harshly dictated the circumstances of people's lives. The daughter, Lily, had a double dose of pride: she always held her head high, had a markedly erect bearing, and came to exert a kind of leadership among the other village girls, from innate superiority of character and intelligence.

She was good-looking, too, with her pale, ivory skin, black

hair and shining black eyes — a little line of want, a slightly sunken look on either cheek. One need hardly ask why — years of under-nourishment; but in those bad old days, when everybody lived near or under subsistence line — except for the classes that ate too much — nobody did ask why.

In any case ours was a free village of tin-miners and china-clay workers: there was no squire to patronise us or squire's lady to recruit the girls into service and thus at least look after them.

Lily's looks and bearing were not lost upon the schoolmaster of the newly established school up the hill, which dominated the other end of the village. Indeed they were a constant stimulus and provocation as the girl approached womanhood.

He, too, had his problem — chiefly, a great deal more sex than he knew what to do with. Now approaching forty, not a good-looking man, he had a roving grey eye, and a large fleshy nose that bespoke his powers. These were still at their height, looking for any likely female outlet, while his wife, many years older than he was, was wizened and dried up. They had had an only son, whom they had educated for the ministry; the wife had refused early in the marriage to have any more children. Poverty, or poor circumstances — for they lived on a mere pittance of a salary and had had to scrape for the son — dictated their lives and made their story for them no less than for the rest of us.

One sees it all now, years after, with compassion. Today it would perhaps not have happened.

Those early days when elementary school education was in its first stages were as restricted in regard to that as in other respects. The working people were not all willing to send their children to school — they wanted them to go to work as soon as possible to help the family. The local School Board had to employ a 'whipper-in' to see that the children attended school.

No such problem in the case of Lily Angwin. She was keen on school, above the average in intelligence. 'Master', as we called him with deference, had his eye on her for a pupil-teacher. There was no question of her going away to college to train: no money for that. Master would take her under his care and tell her all he knew about education — and not only education.

Not that he knew much about that subject himself. A farmer's son from some distance away, he had been sent to a small boarding school and was recruited into teaching after the early School Boards were set up, when there were few teachers as yet to go round.

For much the same reason — and also because he had an early crony in the profession to promote him — he was made a member of the Central School Board at the county town. This gave him a certain aura, and also an excuse to absent himself from school once a month, to attend the Board at Bodmin. We would see him walking early through the village to the station: he had a curious, sideways, slinking way of walking, though he covered the ground quite fast in his grey spats. We were impressed.

Where women were concerned he had an insinuating way. He flattered them; he spoke them fair; he was deferential to them in his amused manner, bright eye glistening with mischief, large sexy nose twitching with desire. This in itself gave him an entrance with them; it was something different from the crudity of approach they were used to from their menfolk.

Unlike really good teachers with a bent for it, he was quite uninterested in the boys. But he made up for it by his interest in the older girls, especially in the better developed ones: instinct, and a little preparatory exploration, told him the ones he could squeeze, stroke, caress, fondle, or go a little further if opportunity offered.

Opportunity didn't offer a lot — it was more teasing than anything else; the girls were usually all together, they came to school and left together; there was always someone about, on the look-out. A few of the more knowing ones recognised Master's little ways.

But with Lily opportunity offered wide open. Instead of leaving school, she remained on as a pupil-teacher, on a pupil-teacher's pittance. Master, as a member of the Board, was able to fix this. She would have done better to go into the town as a milliner and trim hats. Pride forbade; she considered herself above that.

So she taught school for a few years. She was Master's 'favourite' — a category well-recognised in the village. She was grateful:

he had made an opening for her. In return, she made an opening for him.

We didn't know whether any love was involved: both too reserved and careful to let on, Lily too proud and keeping much to herself, Master on a pedestal, not on a level with us for all his little human weakness.

What the village did know was that there was no love lost between Master and his elderly wife. They lived an unhappy life of it. She was a shrew and a crone, in a perpetual ill humour and looked it, with her sallow, wrinkled face and the thunderous expression. Never a smile lit up those twitching eye-brows, so close together as to form one line. We rarely saw her; she didn't choose to know anybody in the village. She could concentrate her talents on making Master's home-life miserable; no doubt he gave her cause to complain. Having nothing else to occupy her, she kept the school-house spotless, not a speck of dust, not a grain or a crumb was left to lie. She was more than thrifty, she was downright mean, watching every penny. The house was swept and garnished, and inhabited by seven devils.

This ill-assorted pair were tied together for their lives, a life-sentence: in those days no means — in both senses of the word — of escape.

No wonder that Master, a perfectly natural, normal man, but more than normally sexed, sought consolation. His wife might rage, look sour, make scenes, but he was inevitably much thrown together with Lily. They were in school together all day. There were 'intervals' or breaks in morning school, and at mid-day dinner time. After school there were the registers to be checked and made up, requisition lists to be made out. Lily was a great help. Master was the only person in the school to have a little room of his own, more of a cubby-hole than a room. He did not seem to make much use of it during school-hours; but it was quite sufficient for his purposes after hours.

Lily must have been quite familiar with its interior. After a few years in those days of ignorance about birth-control, Lily suffered a breakdown. She became thinner, in the cheeks, than before. She went away for a few months to recuperate. She came back with a little baby-girl she had adopted.

Here was progress, a concession to the increasing social sensibility of the time, with the new century. When Lily herself had been born to her unmarried mother, there was no question of her being an adopted child. For the third generation in this gaunt, sad house at the cross-roads, here was a fig-leaf of humbug. This was now the Edwardian age. The village generally adopted the fiction that this was Lily's adopted child; given a rather grand name, Gloria, she was brought up to regard Lily as her adopted mother.

*

The years passed, and Lily, as they used to say, 'lived it down'. After all, we younger people didn't know what had happened before our time; nor would we have fully understood.

The older people did. In particular, an old crone, who did go out to work, was something of a white witch, with her homemade receipts and charms for ailments, and who made it her business to know everybody's business. She knew everything: she had kept watch.

But she was not popular in the village; people were afraid of her sharp tongue, the evil glint in her eye — one of them particularly fierce — and her rough, mannish ways. She was, with her big frame, her strong muscular arms, inured to work, more like a man. Unmarried — she had been brought up to buddle, i.e. wash tin, like a man, at the tin-works. She was not much listened to, except in case of trouble or illness; but she was a 'wise woman'.

There was a certain ambivalence about the paternity of the child. Master's son had been at home on vacation from his first ministry at about the right time; he was just Lily's age, and there were people who thought that he was the father. The son took very much after his father; so Lily's child looked like either: there need be no doubt at any rate about the family relationship. But, growing up, she came to have a curiously older look imprinted on her features — the child of an eldering man.

The 'wise woman' would say, as Master hurried by the little shop month by month, year by year, on his way to the station, keeping as far over as he could to the other side of the road, with his slinking gait in the old grey spats, then striking away from the sad house to take the other road leading to town:

"Ow 'ee can go by that 'ouse like that, an' never once look in, or even look to see 'is own chiel — and Lily Angwin there never so much as lookin' through the window curtain to see'n. W'en what she could say if she d'choose to give tongue!'

She never did choose. She kept herself to herself; she struggled along to keep her mother and her child out of the tiny shop. If anything else came her way, no one ever knew of it. Master kept very much to his end of the village, except for those monthly expeditions past the shop to the station. It must have been the most difficult walk in life for him: though he did not look in that direction, perhaps a pittance passed.

Lily came out of her house very seldom. When she did, her carriage of herself was as erect as ever, head held as high; but life had left its mark on her haggard features, cheeks drawn in upon a stern, proud expression, fine dark eyes sunk in their sockets, the flame still burning.

*

After the war there came to the village a demobilised soldier, a stranger, nobody knew whence or why. He had no relations, no kith or kin, and no business there; nor was there anything for him to do. What had he come there for?

It did not appear that he knew, any more than we did. With his gratuity on being demobbed he came to lodge with Lily and her mother. When that ran out he became an insurance agent: we used to see him making his rounds on his fine new bike, always spick and span, and shining like his bike.

There was a dark glitter about him. He was a handsome enough fellow, with his raven black hair, long, sharp nose, broad heave of shoulders — if it were not for the shifty look in the grey eyes. He simply could not look man or woman straight in the face, or not for any length of time; he just looked away, one's memory of him is that he was perpetually looking away.

Terry was not uppish, however; he was accepted by the village lads, rather than by folk in general, and so rubbed along. After all, he was not much older than the lads, the other fellows who had come back from the war. He was one of them.

He went to lodge with Lily and her mother, and the village was not surprised, after that, at Lily's marrying him. In such situations to have a married name, to be Mrs Crossthwaite, was something of a cover-up for the past. Here was a new start for Lily, a new life was beginning.

Or was it?

Wasn't it rather a new twist in her continuing tragedy?

She can have had no illusions about Terry. She must have soon seen through his superficial charm to the weakness beneath, the shiftlessness, the uncertainty, the life without purpose, or a centre.

To what purpose had his steps been directed to the village, no-one knew whence, or whither he would go?

Lily's head was not turned by her acquisition of a man so much younger than herself. She was not seen about much more than before. After her experience of life she had no illusions about religion and did not attend the local Methodist church to which the village chiefly went.

However, life opened out a little, an effort in a new direction was made. Terry had a good bass voice; he recruited himself to one of the chapels in the neighbouring town that had a good organ and prided itself on its choir. Sometimes, very rarely, Lily would be seen walking through the village of a Sunday evening with Terry on their way to or from chapel. Marriage had made her no more prosperous than before; Terry's earnings were casual and sparse, if he brought in a little, there was one more mouth to feed. Lily appeared in the same old faded hat with the straw brim we had always known; the same coat with the velvet green collar; the same erect carriage of herself, like a duchess.

Then something happened to relieve the strain for a bit. Old Miss Angwin died. One mouth less to feed. But we did not know that some time before Terry had insured her life for a small sum. Nor did we know that shortly before her death Terry had paid a visit to one of the chemists in a neighbouring town.

But the old wise woman had her suspicions. She came to see her neighbour on her death-bed, and within the four walls of her cottage below the village would say:

'I never did see a 'uman bein' die like that — an' I've seen a good many in me time: more like a' animal dyin' from poisonin'.'

That sage person, the local doctor, who had himself put several persons prematurely under the sod by his incompetence, had no suspicions. Old Miss Angwin's death-certificate was signed and in order; she went to her burial without any spreading of rumours. At seventy-five it was time for her to go.

Terry's visit to the chemist's shop was also in order. For he had joined the St John's Ambulance unit, and was a regular member of the local hospital organisation. This gave him some status in our eyes: in his dark blue uniform with the Red Cross on his arm he looked even more sombre and glittering than before.

One dark winter's evening when coming back from ambulance drill in the town, Terry caught up with the clever fat-boy of the village, now launched on adolescence and thinning out into a good-looking boy almost as tall as Terry. They didn't know each other well, but kept each other company along the narrow steep hill out of the town in the friendly country way usual with the villagers.

All the same, the youth was surprised when Terry said in the course of their talk, *à propos* of nothing:

'I could touch you in a certain spot that would kill you in a second.'

The youth was struck by this piece of unsolicited information, and didn't much relish the line of thought it opened up. He said nothing, but he moved instinctively a shade further away from Terry. He remembered the curious challenge in the darkness of the lane when, not a long time after, Terry's first experiment at annihilating life having succeeded so well, he determined on another.

Lily fell ill, and was faithfully attended — her life had also been insured — by Terry. Every time he gave her her

disagreeable medicine she was worse. Younger and tougher
than her mother, she put up a much stronger fight for life. Her
pains were excruciating, her groans could be heard in the road
below her bedroom. Still Terry administered her her medicine;
no one else. She seemed to have no suspicion, while complaining of the bitter taste of the medicine and the agony it gave
her.

Terry consoled her in the age-old formula of the people:
'You must be worse before you are better.'

With her life-long stoicism, dying, she accepted this ancient
wisdom without challenge. She was more concerned in the last
hours of her pitiful life with her daughter than for herself.
Would Terry promise faithfully to look after her? He would —
perhaps he had already formed a plan for her future.

More at peace in mind, though ravaged by the agony she had
been through, Lily called her daughter to her bedside and told
her the truth at last — that she was no adopted daughter but her
own. Even now, proud to the last, faithful to some unknown
promise, loyal to her idea of herself — perhaps, known only to
herself, true to a momentary glimpse of love, long-vanished but
folded and put away for remembrance — she breathed not a
word as to her father.

The kindly doctor, muddled and fuzzy as ever, would have
signed this death-certificate too, if it had not been for the loud
protests of the old crone, the white witch. *She* was not wanting
in courage. She spoke up her mind to all and sundry, that Lily
had been poisoned. She would not be gainsaid.

'Lily Angwin died like 'er mother, like no 'uman bein' I ever
seed. She died the death of a dog. An' it was Terry Pender's
doin', the both of 'em. Poisoned they was, sure as I be alive. An'
I be'n't afraid to say so.'

She made it impossible for the doctor to sign a second death-
certificate, much as he wished to avoid trouble. She said she
would see Terry Pender swing for it.

And swing for it he did.

In later years, such is people's capacity for persuading themselves of anything, the doctor took credit to himself for his discernment in refusing to sign the death-certificate.

What Master thought of these events never transpired. An old man now, with one of those stealthy feet already in the grave, not a word of it all passed his loose and leathery lips.

XVI

The Bishop

The Bishop was a saintly man, and it did him no harm in his impecunious diocese that he was a rich man in his own right. His wealth had come down to him from his grandfather, a Tyneside farmer of yeoman stock on whose land coal had been found. On becoming Bishop in the South he had bought a country estate, with a view of a bay which he was willing to compare with the Bay of Naples. This he knew well, for he was an example of high Victorian culture, much under the influence of Ruskin, and devoted to Italy, which he visited every year – particularly Florence and Rome.

He had inherited a collection of pictures, including a famous Rembrandt, as well as Chinese porcelain from the Summer Palace at Peking, ivories, screens and bronzes.

These, along with potted palms and aspidistras, decorated the large hall of the country house, with dependent estate and the neighbouring farms that went with it.

His idea was to entertain all the clergy of the diocese in turn, and he always had clergy or ordinands staying in the house in that salubrious spot. Sea-air, farm food from the home farm and extensive kitchen garden put many an impoverished and under-nourished parson on his legs again, under the fatherly eye of the good Bishop.

Even more important was their spiritual well-being, the encouragement his devotion gave to the down-hearted and dejected. No intellectual himself, he yet read conscientiously, in the splendid library which his grandfather had begun and his father added to. It contained all four Folios of Shakespeare, the only perfect copy known of Caxton's *Golden Legende* with the Life of St Thomas of Canterbury with it; a first edition of Coverdale's Bible, a unique copy of the York Breviary of 1533, the earliest manuscript of the York Missal; several exquisitely illuminated medieval Books of Hours; rare association copies of Prayer Books and Bibles, including a Prayer Book specially bound in velvet for Queen Elizabeth I. Just the kind of thing that rich Victorian industrialists moving up collected — but a notable collection all the same.

For all his wealth and possessions the Bishop was utterly, and visibly, a humble man. At his enthronement he had declared his wish to be a 'servant of the servants of God', and that he was all his days. He was inspired by the desire to be a true Father in God to clergy and people; and though he was playing no part, he looked it with his noble brow and fine kindly eyes, set off by late Victorian side-whiskers.

In those days it was something to be a bishop — and not a few of them then were distinctly pompous. Indeed their creator, Queen Victoria, declared that she had never known a clergy-man who was not the worse for being made a bishop. She cannot have known Dr Presence — almost certainly not, for he was a High Churchman of the old school, and a Hanoverian, who had taken the place of the Stuarts, she did not approve of that either.

Bishop Presence went on his way, regardless of approval or disapproval: a simple man, doing his duty with all his might.

There was no evidence that he had a sense of humour.

*

The good Bishop had one idiosyncrasy that caused much amusement at his expense, and himself a good deal of trouble. He was so absent-minded that people called him Bishop Absence, and many were the stories told about him.

One well-known one was of his travelling by railway-train, and when the ticket-collector came for his ticket, it couldn't be found.

'It doesn't matter, my lord, you can pay at the other end.'

'But it *does* matter, for without my ticket how do I know where I am going?'

On one occasion a couple of guests arrived a little early for luncheon, to find the Bishop out in the garden. Very pleased to show them his planting, he took them all round; having arrived at the bottom gate, he politely took leave of them and showed them out. They, well aware of the Bishop's little foible, toiled up the hill again and in at the front gate, to present themselves as before. Nothing out of the ordinary for the dear Bishop.

But a garden-party he gave *was* something out of the ordinary. A band was engaged, and a hospitable spread of eatables laid on. The Bishop and his family awaited their guests. No one turned up!

It was then discovered that he had forgotten to send out the invitations.

This little failing endeared him the more to all those who knew him. Though without a sense of humour himself, he was the cause of mirth — and happiness — in others.

Everybody loved him.

*

And everybody took advantage of him.

Farmer Johns farmed the smaller of the two farms in the valley below the estate. Once in a while, when prowling around, he would meet the Bishop out enjoying the morning air.

'Not much luck with the rabbits today, Johns?'

'No, m'lord, not much.'

As the Bishop passed on in meditation, his mind set on higher things, he never noticed the farmer's game-bag, full of his lordship's game-birds.

That didn't prevent Farmer Johns waxing eloquent on the subject of more expert, and more remunerative, 'fernigglers'. 'They were all a lot of fernigglers — ferniggled from morning to night.'

Farmer Johns used to supply the Bishop — as his tenant — hay at £4 a ton. A new coachman taken on fixed up with the next door farmer to provide the Bishop at £3.10 shillings the ton. But he made it only two-thirds of a ton — and those two split the difference.

'The coachman was fool enough to tell the blacksmith at Tristram's Stone. Farmer Johns went down to his erring colleague — 'who was in the mowhay, cutting hay. Never looked up once — you could tell he was guilty.' Next Johns went to the coachman and told him what he knew. 'He cried like rain, and said, if you tell the Bishop it's as much as my place is worth.'

Indoors, 'the cook would order a dozen chickens, ducks, and half-a-dozen pound of fresh butter to be brought — the extra she would send up the line to her friends.' To Farmer Johns, presenting the bill for half-a-dozen pound of butter, she would say,
'Charge for a dozen pound.'
She was well willing to split the difference.
This was how the gentry were diddled, in those days when there were gentry — and servants.

*

The Bishop was an exceptional man, inspired by love and duty. He was dedicated to the idea of fatherhood. Himself had two children — and with Northern patriotism, which he possessed along with old-fashioned Northumbrian courtesy, he named them after those Saints of the North Country: Oswald, and Hilda, after the famous Abbess of Whitby.
The Bishop wrote:

'A father does not, unless in the last extremity, insist upon his rights; he takes them for granted, he recommends them to his children by the love which makes authority more than welcome. So delicate a relationship as that of a father in God does not depend for its working efficacy on the amount of authority which can be arrogated on one side, or on the submission which can be extorted on the other. It depends on moral influences; on the respect which is inspired by high and disinterested character; in the attraction which is exerted by a true love of God and man.'

One of his favourite maxims, which he often urged in sermons or pastoral letters — he was, above all, a pastoral Bishop, not a mere administrator, as so often today — was this:
'A love of children is the heart of aptness to teach them.'
He possessed what was described as 'an Apostolic faith in the capacity of men and women, and boys and girls. Such faith was

rooted in the conviction that God has called each one, and that He will fulfil His call. He was always hopeful of England, never anaemic in his confidence in the nation, never pessimistic.

This was as well, for at that time there fell the South African war — which the historian can see as a foreshadowing of the break-up of the Empire, the ending of the great days of the nation, the decline from the Victorian apogee. There was, at the outset, the 'Black Week' of disasters wrought upon the mighty Empire by the uncompromising, embattled Boers — a small nation of farmers determined on their Old Testament way of life.

The Bishop's optimism was a source of encouragement in those black days. 'I am expecting new gifts to England from the war, not lead or prestige, but character, practical religion and the making of the *jeunesse dorée* into men.'

He did not think of his own son as one of the *jeunesse dorée*, but he was in the Army in South Africa and the Bishop would speak of him with pride.

He was indeed 'a very present help in trouble' — to quote the Psalms — to all and sundry, but especially to those whose sons were in danger, or sick, or wounded. 'I am daily thinking of you both', he wrote to two such anxious parents, 'and I have begun to remember your Noon Intercession in Cathedral, which is easy enough, as my wife and I are always in our chapel at that time when I am at home.'

To the proud parents of a winner of the VC — 'With all our growth of knowledge we have not yet learnt how much of a son's distinction is woven out of hereditary qualities, and, however much the child has to work them up, the raw material must have dwelt considerably in his father and mother.'

*

He had reason to reflect on this when his own son returned, after three years in South Africa, a Major, but a confirmed drunkard, in the initial stages of DT. The Bishop spoke of him no more around the estate. Farmer Johns:

'When he came home, he revealed himself the drunken fool he was. He used to stammer, and beat his sides, and stamp his foot to get his words out. If you looked at him he couldn't speak at all.'

When he came down to the place he would send for Farmer Johns to go out rabbiting with him. One such day he went up:

'After lunch there was a perfect downpour. And he wanted me to go shootin' pheasants with him. I wouldn' go shootin' no pheasants. For then he'd know I could shoot. I didn't want him to know I could shoot. Whereas I *'ad* shot scores of 'em.

After the Bishop's death, it didn't take Major Oswald long to run through the estate. The place abounded in drink. It was nothin' for all the servants to be drunk and the Master upstairs having DT. Bit by bit all the Bishop's cherished pictures, books, and possessions were sold. The butler would be sent up to London with a couple of pictures to sell.'

He would say to Farmer Johns,
   'I've got a picture worth £20,000 to take up next week.'
   The Farmer put a couple of thousand on it — out of which the butler would get his share.
   Thus the Rembrandt went; so with the majolica, Chinese vases, screens, books, etc. Until the place itself was sold: to become — in a society which regards mental defectives as more important than mental effectives — a home for mental defectives.
   In spite of what the Bishop thought, or thought he thought, ordinary people — whatever class they come from — are apt to be poor stuff.

XVII

The Inheritor

In East Cornwall not far from the Devon Border was a very cosy little estate, nice to inherit, by name Menadue, i.e. dark rocks. These same rocks rose high above the estate, sheltered in the valley below; from them one could see far off the entrance to the Hamoaze, Plymouth harbour, and indeed in those days — round about 1800 — St Vincent's or Nelson's fleet under sail coming in from on guard in the Channel. Those were the years of the war against Napoleon, that meant so much to the imagination of Thomas Hardy, as indeed to the folk along the Channel coast at the time.

The family at Menadue had the good old name of Hender (actually meaning 'the old place'), and consisted of parents with five children: two sons and three young daughters. The elder of the two boys was to inherit, and was left to country pursuits, those proper to a young gentleman growing up.

What to do with the younger, but to make him a lawyer, able to carve out a career for himself? Also not without a contingent utility for any law business arising from the estate — terms of leases, the complexities and disputes that came from the system that predominated in Cornwall then — leases on three lives.

Young Richard Hender was thereupon articled, willy nilly, to a well known attorney at St Austle (as it was spelt then), who had business all over the county — let us call him Mr Duporth.

It might have been foretold that Hender had no interest in or aptitude for the law. However, Mr Duporth, who had an eye for a personable young fellow, took an interest in him and gave him more latitude than might have been expected. Besides, the lawyer knew the family, without being intimate with it, occasionally transacted some business for it, concerning its town property in Plymouth, ground rents and such.

In those days every scrap of legal business was transacted long hand, often enough on expensive parchment, with all the paraphernalia of red wax seals etc. There fell a great deal of copying to the two clerks articled to Mr Duporth, and it did not take him long to observe how utterly bored young Richard was with it.

The attorney was willing enough to make allowances for the gentleman of the two, whom he regarded with favour. Without being good-looking, Hender was a well set up fellow, good with his hands and muscles, if not with his head. Mr Duporth noticed how handy he was about the place, with his horses, in the stables, knowledgeable enough about carpentry, repairs and so on.

So, to give him some reprieve from endless copying, Mr Duporth gave him time off to help with his boats in the little harbour he had himself created to serve the local tin and copper mines in which he had interest.

'You don't care much for the law, do you?' he said one day when they were down at the harbour together.

Hender flushed a little at so direct an impeachment; though it was obvious enough, he wondered what might come next, for − although not quick in the uptake − he was not unaware of his patron's special interest in him. Utterly unresponsive, he did not welcome being singled out in this way; his fellow clerk noticed the attention Hender received and had commented on it, rather embarrassingly. He had got no change − and neither had the master.

Hender eventually got round, after a pause for some thought, to admitting:

'No, sir, rightly speaking, I don't.'

'You prefer messing round with boats?'

Richard's interest in this quarter could not be denied; it needed no comment.

'And not only with boats,' added the master.

It had not escaped his observant eye that Richard took every opportunity that afforded to cross the ancient Bull Ring in front of Mr Duporth's spacious house-cum-office, round the corner into High Cross Street, at the bottom of which stood the hardly less spacious establishment of the local doctor, physician and surgeon.

The doctor kept a couple of maids, in one of whom the young gentleman was much interested. It was only a step around the corner, and up the lane to the back of the doctor's premises, the kitchen court where often enough Richard could get sight of his kitchen maid.

Margy was a few years older than the gentleman, and in truth further acquainted with the facts of life than he was, not averse to being noticed by someone of superior station — the lawyer to be (or not to be). In short, a stronger personality for all her lack of education — not only innocent of an 'h', but incapable of pronouncing it — she led him on. Dark, blazing eyes, wavy hair drawn back from broad forehead, there was something mysterious about her that held him: he longed to penetrate further.

They made ways and means of meeting, and — not to make too fine a point of it — he was caught and became thoroughly besotted.

News of the young gentleman's entanglement with someone so unsuitable — a couple of classes below him — got about, and it did not take long before Mr Duporth carpeted the youth. He represented to him the impropriety of such an attachment, the impossibility of its coming to any good. What would his family think, when it came to their ears?

He was surprised by the obstinacy he met with in one so young, and — as he considered — so unformed. Clever man as he was, he did not allow for an element of sullenness in Hender, a hardly conscious resentment at the older man's attitude towards him — what was it? What was it intended to lead up to? Was there some design behind that designing legal brain, which he could never quite make out, let alone fathom?

Faced with an absolute refusal of the young man to drop the girl, the lawyer felt it his duty — though there was an element of mingled resentment and pleasure in his doing so — to report the situation to the family.

Then the fat was in the fire — resentment spilled over in all directions. Absolute opposition from parents at home: the threat from his father to cut off the allowance upon which Richard was subsisting, to refuse the completion of the articles upon which were based the hope of a future career; reproaches from his mother at the disgrace to his family — fancy proposing to marry a servant-girl!

Nothing moved the infatuated youth. After all, he had no fancy for the career proposed for — or, he felt rather, imposed upon — him. As for the estate, what did it matter to him? He was only a younger son, his brother was the heir.

A complete *non-possumus* was arrived at in the attorney's view — unless he could find means of breaking it. He felt that it rested with him to do so: he did not relish being outfaced by a youngster, where his particular inclinations had received no response other than sullen resentment.

Hender would not yield, held to it that he would marry the girl in spite of all.

It was then that Mr Duporth played his trump card. He had set on foot a few quiet inquiries. It was not long before he discovered the mystery in the girl's background: in the background she had an illegitimate child.

It gave him some pleasure to impart the news to his young reprobate, who took the revelation as the blow it was meant to be. A blow at the most vulnerable point in the masculine make-up — male pride. He had thought himself first in that pristine field, he had the uninitiated youth's conviction of woman's innocence — now he had penetrated the withheld mystery that had so seduced him.

It was then that *he* played an unexpected hand. The house of cards, his fabric of illusion crumbled within him, he disappeared — disappeared completely. He was never heard of again in the vicinity, or in the county, so long as he lived.

In those days it was an easier matter to disappear — though even today people unknown disappear at the hands of murderers society should discard, enemies of the human race.

During the long war against the French Revolution and Napoleon — with the superfluous war with the new United States on top of it all — a man might be lost on land or at sea, at home or abroad, in any of those wars. It was assumed, after some years had elapsed and nothing whatever was heard of him — no light on *that* mystery — that he was dead. His family gave up all hope of him, and assumed as much.

What happened in fact was much odder.

It transpired many years later that he made his way to Liverpool, and there lived under an assumed name. Since all he possessed went into a small trunk with the initials R.H., he kept to the initials but called himself Roger Henwood.

It is curious that families of a certain standing expect their offspring to be intelligent. But it is not normal to be intelligent: to be intelligent indeed is an abnormal condition for ordinary humans. And Richard Hender, of that old family, lapsed into being what Roger Henwood was – a handyman.

He had always been good with his hands. He became a tradesman, as a carpenter. He sank into a working-class way of life which was, perhaps after all, more in keeping with his nature than that to which he was born and the career intended for him – perhaps his original falling for a servant-girl indicated that.

At any rate he married another, by whom he had a couple of children, a boy and a girl. They lived quietly in a back street in Liverpool, where he made one or two shifts in his work – always something manual, quasi-mechanical – wheelwright, then shipwright.

Eventually he took on a job as lock-gate keeper on the newly opened Runcorn-Manchester Canal. There one day he as quietly slipped – quite accidentally – into the Canal and was drowned.

He had never mentioned his people to his family, or spoken of his background, betrayed his past or that he knew Cornwall. It was only upon his death that the facts came to light from the papers he kept locked in his R.H. trunk.

Inquiries were set on foot, with the aid of the local solicitor, from which the little family learned that they were the undoubted heirs to the Menadue estate. The elder brother had died unmarried, and for years the estate had supported the three sisters who had lived there together: now old spinsters rejoicing in the names Eulalia, Tryphena, Eugenia.

So 'Roger Henwood' had been the true heir on the death of his brother, and now his son Henry 'Henwood' was in fact the inheritor.

A case was submitted to the Assize Court in Cornwall, in those days at Launceston, and a posse of witnesses was summoned to give evidence. They were not even called, the evidence was so clear in itself.

The family transferred itself to Menadue, agreement being arrived at for a modest maintenance being provided for the ageing aunts. Something of a compromise was arrived at by the incoming nephew, who felt himself not quite up to making the complete transition to the rank his father had been born to. So he compromised by hyphenating his name, since he had been registered as Henwood, and called himself Hender-Henwood, the next generation reverting to the true original.

XVIII

The Amateur Archaeologist

What was this Englishman of indeterminate age — shall we say, approaching early middle age — doing earning his living (if that is the word for it), a mere pittance, hardly enough to keep body and soul together, in the slums of Trastevere? It was unexpected, to say the least, of someone who had had a good Public School and Oxford education, not to mention a respectable family background — all which had gained him an early posting in the consular service, with further prospects of a move into the diplomatic ranks. The prospects had been good, for he was exceptionally good at languages.

But no. For anyone tactless enough to put the point — fortunately he hardly ever met nowadays anyone who knew his background, let alone his story — he would have had an answer: that he preferred to live his life this way.

Improbable as it would seem, it was in accordance with the evidence — the ocular evidence at least.

He inhabited a largish room in a squalid little court round a turning off the piazza in front of San Francesco a Ripa. Appropriately in a way, for this had been the site of St Francis of Assisi's first little monastic establishment and of his labours among the poor.

Was it the name that had drawn him there, for he too was a Francis—? Was it sub-conscious, drawn thither after some self-revelation, some trauma? Or penance? It was hardly that — more that he too liked the company of the poor, particularly the *giovine*, of that slum area, though for other reasons than those of the saint.

The boys were constantly in and out of his premises, helping themselves to what scraps of food that were going — he usually had a saucepan on his gas-ring, into which he put bits of meat, pasta, cheese, vegetables: a savoury mess that met his needs as it did theirs. He liked their gaiety, their spirit, their mercurial temperament − even the explosions did something for him, he could hardly say what. Perhaps it lifted him out of the melancholy that was below the surface − that never emerged above the surface when they were about.

Was the word 'liking' sufficient to describe his relations with them? He certainly liked them, and from time to time there were favourites whom he more than liked. But relations were at a less conscious level − he no longer put the matter to himself: he accepted them, though years older he had become one with them, lived on their level. That was why he was there.

Perhaps a modern version of going to the poor like his namesake six centuries before? − Hardly, for the motive was different; it was certainly not religious; nor had it been voluntary.

Nor was he a St Francis in physical type. He was tall and gangling, strikingly dark for an Englishman with sympathetic, slightly bovine, dark eyes. This enabled him to melt into the environment − except for his height, and the ancient grey flannel trousers and blazer he usually wore with his frayed sporting jacket: an English enough outfit.

One other feature added an air of oddity: not yet greying, he had a white-lock that drew attention to his broad forehead. He was rather a fine figure of a man, with a curious air of distinction, of having seen better days.

This was true. Moreover, he was accident-prone. At school, in camp, during OTC training he had been the one to fall off an army-lorry and break his leg. Taking to riding − though no figure for it, legs far too long − he had fallen off his horse and fractured thigh and ribs.

But one accident he might have incurred he managed to avoid.

On his arrival in Rome from Naples, late one night at Easter time, he had had difficulty in getting a room, and at length settled for a dubious little *pensione* indeed, kept by a couple whose looks gave him the gravest suspicions. They led him to a back room which, he noticed, had no lock on the door, no key, no means of fastening it from inside.

However, needs must. He moved the washstand up against the door, trigging it firmly against the door handle. Sure enough, in the night he heard furtive fingers trying the handle. In the morning, looking out of the window, he saw that it gave straight on to the Tiber: a convenient drop, an easy disposal of a body.

*

The sight of the water made him shudder.

His permanent room — so far as anything was permanent in his make-shift life — was a little way in from the Tiber with no view of it at all. Looking down upon the smelly little court, it had one pleasant feature, a balcony which gradually he filled with plants and flowers. From thence the youths could chatter with their friends below, squirt — or occasionally make — water on their enemies.

If the term were not already out of date, one would say that the establishment was a pre-hippy one.

How did he manage to make ends meet, food-wise? His sexual needs were catered for. And he never got mugged — as he certainly would have been in the *pensione*'s dank room overlooking the Tiber.

The friendly relations he enjoyed with the youth of the court protected him; besides, nothing in his bare room was worth taking — they could hardly steal his tumbled bed, already common property. A table, a cupboard, a few sticks of chairs — anything else they were free of; his food, whatever was going, he gladly shared. Perhaps even the word 'gladly' is too precise: he accepted the fact, like his lot. They all mucked in together: it made a life, of a sort, and he had lost hope.

There must have been a pittance from somewhere, perhaps his family, or he would have starved. But he made some money on the side, in an interesting way. Earlier, before fate overtook him, he had cultivated an interest in archaeology; he was only an amateur, but this came in handy. In the tourist season, from spring to autumn, he turned guide to parties of tourists, especially Americans, avid of knowledge in a simple packaged form, and they were generous with their tips. And sometimes a little curious. They got no further.

All Rome was his parish, and he was always available: nothing else in view. But right on his doorstep in Trastevere there was plenty for him to show tourists, when his luck was in.

Just round the corner was there not the famous Santa Cecilia in Trastevere, founded on the site of the house where the Saint had lived? Fascinating within, with its frescoes and recumbent figure of the lady by Maderna, was not her very bathroom preserved, in which she had been tortured by scalding before being beheaded?

Below the church were delights that appealed even more to the amateur archaeologist − not so much a crypt, as a lower, earlier church, as so often in Rome. This was the sepulchral chapel of the Saint, to which her remains had been brought by an early Pope from the catacombs.

To the archaeologist's delight the lower building was pre-Christian: an ancient tannery, a niche in the wall with a little figure of Minerva, patroness of handicrafts. On his visits he paid his respects to the pagan deity rather than to the Saint.

Everywhere in his neighbourhood were such amenities, which it amused him to expound − and watch the reactions from his auditors, credulous or incredulous, simple or sophisticated, hardly ever the last. He was especially amused, among Italians, with their mixture of credulity and scepticism.

One day, at the tail-end of a party, there arose a vivacious dispute, in the Italian manner, which gave him much amusement − it so corroborated his contempt for people's prejudices, even for human 'thinking'. Further, it illustrated the difference between the sexes in regard to thinking, what little regard women had for truth. It fed his misogyny.

A lay-sister in a habit was holding forth to the couple she was accompanying, about the Holy House of Loreto. The Blessed Virgin's house at Nazareth, in which she had received the Annunciation, had been levitated six inches from the ground.

'Impossible,' said the man in the group, evidently husband and brother, or brother-in-law.

'Oh, yes it had,' said the sister with conviction, and gave the exact measurements. 'Not only that, but the angels transported it all the way across the sea from Nazareth, until it came to rest at Loreto.'

'Ridiculous,' said the man.

'But you can *see* the house for yourself. I have *seen* it at Loreto.'

The dispute waxed hot, each holding his or her own ground. The only concession the religious would make to secular rationality was that the house was a 'very little one'. Even so, the angels could transport anything.

Rather than let the dispute go any further, the wife weighed in to keep the peace, repeating:

'*C'è un miracolo. C'è un miracolo.*'

Francis registered that she didn't care any more than the other woman whether it was true or not. Peace was more important — another feminine trait.

*

Such episodes added spice to his daily bread. Not that his daily round in the tourist season lacked interest for him, archaeological even more than human. (He liked archaeology better than people.)

Everywhere in the churches round were frescoes, mosaics, *cosmati* pavements to delight the eye.

Santa Maria in Trastevere was founded on the spot where a miraculous well of oil had gushed forth at the very moment of Christ's birth. The interior especially pleased Francis, for the nave was carried upon a score of ancient Ionic columns from the Baths of Caracalla — a favourite reprobate with him — and they had originally been decorated by the heads of Egyptian deities.

The little church of Santa Maria dell'Orto had been partly built by Julio Romano, the only artist of the time to have been mentioned by name by Shakespeare.

The fact that Francis knew that and drew attentions to it brought him a welcome (if temporary) access of fortune. It appealed to the sentimental heart of an American professor, whose job it was to 'teach Shakespeare' in a well-heeled Liberal Arts College. He procured a useful little lecture-tour assignment for Francis one winter-semester, which gave him a visit to the States, and a little cash over to fall back on.

Not that Francis was any good at holding on to it. Nor did the promising acquaintance last. Though a bachelor, whose tastes were much the same as Francis', if not wholly so, the professor was more than discreet: repressed, *bien pensant*, a Southern Puritan — than whom there can be none more pure — he had, in Francis' phrase, 'gone to the good'. Francis had gone to the bad, and — accident-prone as ever — had told him his story.

*

Francis was posted to Naples when the war was ending, Southern Italy in Allied occupation, the harbour packed with craft large and small, American and British, warships, transports, troopships, carriers.

War is a great stimulus to the passions, a free-for-all — and a fine time was had by all. However, even a game, at a certain level of expertise, has to be played by the rules.

One evening, on board a British destroyer, a party was given at which Francis, temporarily seconded to the Consular Office, met a young midshipman from his home town in the West Country. Here was a bond of mutual interest. Mutual attraction followed. It was arranged that the young West Countryman should have shore-leave next evening — to return sharp for duty at 6 a.m.

The evening was spent agreeably at one of the little *trattorie* Francis knew, not far from the slopes beneath Sant Elmo and his own flat, where they spent the night blissfully.

Indeed they overslept. It was already nearing 6 a.m. when Francis awoke. Hurrying his young compatriot into his fast little sports car, they sped down the awakening streets to the harbour area, and out on the long narrow Molo San Vincenzo, where the destroyer lay alongside.

On a patch of oil-slick the car skidded, into the water.

Francis never knew rightly how he surfaced. His young companion never did.

There was of course an inquiry. Little was to be said; and, in the discreet British way, little was said. Francis was asked to resign, his promising career at an end.

Such was the story his professor acquaintance learned, with disapproval. The acquaintanceship came to an end. So, shortly, did the cash.

Francis came back to his insalubrious quarters in Trastevere, and his hand-to-mouth existence. After all, if all resources gave out, there was always, just around the corner, the Tiber.

XIX

How our College came to be Founded

We are very proud of our agricultural college — 'cow colleges'
they used to call them in the United States a century ago. But a
jolly sight more useful they are than modern mushroom universities, where the professors can't write and the students can't
even read, and all want to 'do' sociology anyway. Which merely
means shooting their mouths off about current affairs, when
they haven't enough experience of life to qualify even to have an
opinion. At that time of life they should be laying in the foun-
dations of knowledge, learning the grammar and discipline of a
subject.

That is what our agricultural students are doing at Sawle-
Harris College — as one could see from a visit to it the other day.
There they were, a fine upstanding lot of farmers' sons, com-
plexions as healthy and ruddy as the red-soil part of the West
Country they were reared in. Moreover, their hair was properly
cut and attended to, tidy and shapely to the head — instead of
the scruffy mass of hair and shapeless beards of university
students, out of which they peer like owls, blinking in broad
daylight. One wouldn't think they ever took in a draft of fresh
air.

Sawle-Harris stands on the edge of moorland, just where the
Moor comes down to meet the rich red soil of the southern
hundreds towards the sea — the air breathing heather and fresh
bracken, ling and the tang of camomile, occasionally a good
sharp whiff from cow-byre or lay-stall, farmyard or barnyard
hay.

The College was on the edge of what had been a large estate
in Victorian times, and Mr Dunsford was a very rich man in
land, a squire of many broad acres.

Himself was not a broad, well set up man, but lean and

hungry-looking, with a melancholy look of the perpetually unsatisfied about him.

And no wonder. For he was the last of his race — and a bachelor, through no fault of his own. He had done his best to amend matters — twice over, as a matter of fact. He was of a loyal nature, with an unsuspected streak of imagination beneath that unprepossessing exterior: he did what no one else would have done. Leastways, what no one else I have heard of *has* done.

He was very much in love with the choosy daughter of a neighbouring squire, a rather handsome piece, Christian Hansford, erect and tall, with the taking combination of dark hair and very blue eyes.

She could not fancy him, and married an impecunious fellow, of much better looks — and probable potency — one Sawle-Harris. They produced a son. After this effort, the husband died.

Mr Dunsford again asked her to marry him; again she rejected him, not too unkindly — though, shortly after, she married another.

*

The boy, Martin, turned out very like his mother, tall, with the same black hair and violet eyes. When Mr Dunsford died, he left his whole fortune to Martin, who reminded him so much of his mother, when young.

Martin was much ogled and pursued by the ladies of the county — particularly by mothers with daughters to marry. The combination of his fortune, his personable looks, and availability, made him the chief target of the county, the marked down and destined victim of the hunt.

The pursuit was on. But they found that Sawle-Harris was not as available as they thought.

He had the less difficulty in escaping their clutches in that he turned out a non-marrying sort. He had been early, and regularly, initiated into the facts of life by the headmaster of the small boarding school his parents had sent him to, and that had set him in his ways, his tastes leaning anyway in that direction.

(The Victorians were better acquainted with that side of life than modern sexologists suppose.)

Still, he avoided unpleasantness by escaping to London, where he lived in much bachelor comfort, and no domestic troubles, in a large house in Victorian Belgravia.

But not alone. He took up to live with him the handsome son of one of the farmers on his estate, a likely lad of sixteen, whom his father had taken away from the same small school to run his farm.

Here the squire grew acquainted with him, fell for him and took him up to London as companion, adopted son, or what you will, to live amicably and agreeably, in considerable style.

*

One day Mr Sawle-Harris said to his young companion, now a grown man of twenty-one:

'I've been thinking — I think I must go and see my lawyer.'

They went together in the carriage into the City. While Martin waited, Mr Sawle-Harris went up and gave instructions for a codicil to his will, leaving everything to Martin.

Next morning Mr Sawle-Harris was found dead in bed.

The butler came to Martin's room:

'What are we to do?'

Martin didn't know; he had no idea about the will. Ingenuous — this was part of his attraction — not at all designing or even expectant, he had never given the matter thought. His benefactor's death was quite unexpected; it had come suddenly, a shock to them all.

It was the butler, practical man, who said,

'There must be a will, sir.'

'I suppose so, but I know nothing about it. He never mentioned it.'

'If you could put your hand on it, sir, it would provide instructions.'

'But I have no idea where it would be.'

Pause. Then the butler:

'What about the lawyer, sir?'

Martin didn't know the name of the lawyer, and had not been

up to his chambers with Mr Sawle-Harris. He then thought of
the coachman: *he* would know, he had taken them into the
City.

*

Martin returned on their tracks. The lawyer said:

'You're a lucky young man: he has left everything to you.'

But the codicil changing the disposition of the estate had not
been signed.

The full will had provided that the first purpose of the estate,
whatever subsequent dispositions might be made, was to be a
foundation for the public benefit in or near the West Country
estates.

On the other hand, there was no doubt what the last intention of the testator had been.

This took a good deal of sorting out. The young fellow, not in
the least grasping or aggressive, wasn't going to contest his
benefactor's will. After much (expensive) consultation with the
experts, a nice compromise was arrived at: it was decided that
both will and codicil (in part) should be honoured.

And so the bulk of the estate did not fall into the hands of the
lucky young man: it went into the founding of the College for
young farmers of which we are so proud.

There was still enough of the large estate for Martin to marry
on — though whether *that* was in accord with his benefactor's
wishes or intentions or foresight, history does not say.

Martin did, however, inherit — along with a competence for
life — his benefactor's public spirit. He cooperated fully in the
founding of the College, saw to it that it bore its benefactor's
name — though few knew the whole story behind it. He returned
to the West Country and farming, and took a life-long interest
in the College as a governor.

XX

The Nibbled Bread

The house was a vicarage, and it was situated — as medieval houses were apt to be — deep in a valley, for water and shelter. It was already a mysterious enough situation, the house looking up against a hill, so that it did not get any sun until nearly midday. And it was in the rather lost part of central Wales, woods and streams, only one road running across ancient 'Forest' to the coast.

The new incumbent's family had been installed there for only a little time when they noticed a curious phenomenon, of no particular significance. It was the suddenness, and the regularity, of the interference that drew their attention to it, so that they could tell when it began. Wherever they left the bread overnight in the kitchen, by morning it was nibbled all round the crust.

Obviously — mice, they thought.

But there were no mice. Even so, they introduced a cat, to be on the safe side.

The nibbling continued.

Could it be birds? One has known birds to attack books, paperbacks or book-jackets — robins especially, coming in through an open window, will attack books with ferocity at certain times of the year. Nesting-time? But few birds were about, and none observed to come indoors.

The scope of observation was narrowed down, and watch kept by the two sons, who didn't believe in the phenomenon. The women had no such difficulty from prosaic rationalist preconceptions: they knew better than to impose a rigid formula of consistency and regularity upon the variability, the unpredictability, of life.

The brothers decided that it must be bats — though they had

never heard of bats nibbling bread. Though there were bats in the belfry of the church nearby, there was no sign of bats in the house, nor did any of the family ever see one.

However, the young men decided to lock the bread away in the safe, so that it could *not* be nibbled by bats, any more than by rats, or mice, or birds, or possibly the cat.

Next morning, they found the bread nibbled as before.

*

They decided to keep watch.

The kitchen had two windows, at right angles to each other. The brothers waited there in the wavering uncertain light of evening, at the approach of night, when the odd event regularly happened.

They waited and waited.

Nothing.

They were bored, growing impatient and feeling rather foolish, when they heard an odd noise.

What was it? Steps? But it was not like footsteps.

They could not resist going out.

Nothing. Only the old dog they had taken over with the house, beating his tail wildly with pleasure. You know how a dog beats his tail unnoticing, oblivious of anything it might knock over − unlike a cat.

That must have been the odd noise they had heard, like a heart pounding away. Nothing more. Nothing different.

Or was there nothing different?

For in that moment of absence, of dereliction from their self-imposed duty, the windows had been left unwatched for a few minutes.

And in those minutes the bread had been interfered with, nibbled all round. So there was some *interference*, and it was from outside.

The '*outside*' world. But was it outside? How does one know what is outside from what is within? Was this a fragment of a world of illusion − fragmented from a collective illusion?

The family had divided on the issue. Now the brothers had to admit that the rest of the family *may* have been right after all.

But what did the others think? They did not know what to think. Rationalism had been defeated, but no more had they an answer.

The mother determined to consult another, a rival source of knowledge — a malign one.

She called up — or perhaps one should say, in — the old sexton of the parish. He was a satyr of a man. Rumour had it that he had starved his wife to death, and that she had actually died — incredibly — for want of bread.

When the troglodyte of a sexton came to the vicarage, the new incumbent's wife put the question to him directly. He stopped in his tracks, his eyes upon her suspiciously, a gleam of perception of strange things lurking in their green depths. He then shot out an enigmatic sentence:

'What began so suddenly shall as suddenly have an end.'

He himself looked changed all of a sudden — strength gone out of him, he looked very old and ill. The vicar's wife thought that he would have tottered.

But no — head bent, as if he had received a blow — he made his way out of the house.

Then she heard the sound of a fall: he had fallen down the steps outside — dead.

With his death there was never any more nibbling of the bread. Whatever spirits were abroad were appeased. The trouble was at an end.

The newcomers inquired a little further into this sinister character. But little could they learn from the scattered parishioners, living their own lives to themselves in that remote, shut-in valley, retaining their secrets and not willing to reveal those of their own people to strangers.

All that these could learn was that the old sexton, who was also verger and looked after the church — diminutive and little frequented (the parish was mostly Welsh Calvinist) — was very miserly, and had an odd fixation about bread. He would rarely buy any, but collected odds and ends of church-bread left over from the Communion.

Now that was against both Canon Law and Rubric, by which the consecrated bread left over should be consumed then and there by the priest officiating at the service. None should be left, which might — as everyone knew — be used for purposes of witchcraft.

But what did he — so familiar with the holy Elements of bread and wine as to become a familiar himself — care about Canon Law or Rubric?

XXI

Psalm 109

My story is a true one (as Thomas Hardy's were), merely fleshed out with the knowledge of the time and place, with some understanding of our peculiar Cornish character.

The time in this instance was the 1770's, the threshold of the war with our own kith and kin — the American colonies, to become the United States. The place was a rocky parish in the far west of Cornwall; the characters stood in some contrast with each other. The young woman in question was as rocky and precipitous as her native parish of Zennor; her young man as level as the plateau beneath the churchtown, the depression below the inland heights, rather featureless above the cliffs — and then, the steep drop to the sea.

The young couple — for such they appeared and were regarded as such by everybody — were first cousins. In those static, immobile days, when few people went far from the bounds of their native parish — unless they went to sea — there was a good deal of inbreeding in these remote localities. And, in fact, in the background of the family there was a strain of insanity, at least mental debility.

Perhaps it was this that kept young Tom Combe from taking the final step and marrying his cousin Elizabeth outright. For they were regarded as engaged, and regarded so by themselves.

But Tom never announced the day. Elizabeth felt this as a slur on her, and took the postponement with mounting impatience. So also did the parish, in so small a district where everybody knew everybody else's business.

However, the family inheritance came out in the two cousins in markedly different ways. Elizabeth was all impatience, rather hoity-toity, gave herself airs, was very demanding. Tom was too sensitive, easily depressed and dejected, but could not be brought up to the mark.

'You may bring a horse to the water,' said the parish, 'but you can't maak'n drink.'

The situation got on Elizabeth's nerves, and she was a 'nervy' type as we say. She kept pressing that he should say the word — she expected it, and so did the parish. People talked, and this was the cause of a breach.

The breach worsened things, for Elizabeth knew that people were gossiping behind their backs, especially when the parish came together at church on Sundays.

For they were a Church-going family. When the 22nd of the month came round and Psalm 109 came to be read in the course of Morning Prayer, Elizabeth took it sharply home to herself and her condition.

> Hold not thy tongue, O God, . . . for the mouth
>   of the deceitful is opened upon me . . .
> For the love that I had . . . lo, now they take
>   the contrary part.
> Thus have they rewarded me evil for good,
>   and hatred for my good will.

We should say, in modern parlance, that an element of persecution mania crept into her state of mind: she felt confirmed in her suspicion as the Psalm continued:

> O deliver me, for I am helpless and poor,
>   and my heart is wounded within me. . . .
> I became also a reproach unto them: they
>   that looked upon me shaked their heads.

Still, it was not only she that was helpless and poor — Tom was too: he simply could not offer her a home as yet — and time went on.

Her reproaches became more vehement, and she drew Tom's attention to the expression of her feelings in the Psalm. She flung it in his face, with imprecations that at length angered him; slow-coach as he was, even mulish, he had the testiness of a mule, and replied in kind.

Elizabeth's return was that she would rather die than go on like this, she would rather kill herself.

Vexed with these constant refrains and tiffs between them, Tom turned to another girl for consolation. What else? Perhaps his attentions to a more cheerful type, that made no demands — as yet — were not wholly serious, but the parish noted the new move. The tide of talk rose higher. The effect on Elizabeth was more than serious.

What called more attention to the breach was that the new girl with whom Tom was 'walking out' was a Chapel girl. One Sunday at the end of May month she prevailed on him to escort her in form to the Wesleyan Chapel. The Combes were Church people. The parish took this new development as portending a serious intention.

So did Elizabeth. She took her Prayer Book, folded down the leaf at Psalm 109, left it open on the kitchen table, went out into the field and hanged herself.

Returning to the close proximity of the village Tom inquired for his cousin, since she had not been seen all that Sunday, nor had been at Church. Entering her cottage, familiarly as of old, he noticed the open Prayer Book, read the Psalm where the leaf was turned down — and with an instant pang of intuition, closeness of family inheritance, or whatever, he realised that she had carried out her threat.

And, of course, the parish blamed him.

He could not face the reproaches he saw on people's faces, the way they avoided him, and what some of the more loud-mouthed openly said to him.

He left his native village in black depression of mind and went to live at Penzance. Here he attended church in old St Mary's chapel, at the bottom of Chapel Street — though never on the 22nd of the month, when the horror of Psalm 109 with its fatal memory might rise up to accuse him. For it preyed on his mind enough, without going to church to hear it confirmed. Nor would he go near the Church school lest he should hear it read.

He worked at intervals in the mines along the coast in West

Penwith, and suffered several injuries in the course of his work, the dangers of those days when there were hundreds of feet of ladders to go up and down, and the workings went out under the sea: the poor fellows could hear the crash and rumble of the rocks as they were moved about on the sea-floor overhead.

Tom regularly imputed the hurts he received at work to the curse he felt his cousin had threatened if he left her. In sleep he saw her face again as after her death – (the mark round her neck, in Hardy's remorseless phrase of a hanged man, 'the colour of a ripe blackberry'). He would cry out in his sleep,

'Shut the book! Shut the book!'

Eventually he came to think that, if he did marry, family responsibility might take the place of – or at least erode – the obsession that was always awaiting him just around the corner of his mind.

Several women who knew his story – the Psalm and its curse upon him – rejected him out of hand. At length one girl was brave enough to face the risk in taking him.

All was fixed for a quiet wedding in a country church. They were on the road when the little party was overtaken by a tremendous hurricane. They managed to get to the church, within its enclosure of swaying and roaring trees, but in fine disarray and soaked to the skin. Worse, the bridegroom was convinced that this was the curse upon him all over again. He was terrified, married in fear and trembling, teeth chattering so that he could hardly make the responses.

Though he fathered two children, the curse did not fall on them – 'let his children be fatherless' – for they died in infancy. And it was only a couple of years before he followed them. His mind in a constant state of depression, he died aged only thirty-seven, before the year 1780 was out or the American war had ended.

But what was curious again – as if there were some fatality about it, or at least a malign consistency: while his body lay in the church for burial, the 22nd of the month came round and Psalm 109 was read over him again. Local people, whose minds were alert to such coincidences, noticed that the poor man's body was buried on a Sunday at 4 in the afternoon, the hour at which his cousin Elizabeth — his first girl and, in a sense, the one who was with him to the last — had killed herself.

XXII

Miss Tryphena and Miss Euphemia

'What do you girls think you are doing? Up at this unearthly hour! Having rigs of fun, I suppose – and eating my nice buns, I see!'

The girls' giggles died away from the lamp-lit kitchen-table as they looked up and saw the spectre of the senior, the more formidable, of the two maiden ladies, their mistress, glaring at them from the doorway. There she was, booming at them in her deep man's voice, in her nightgown padded and quilted against winter, gold spectacles quivering with anger on her nose.

She always seemed to be angry – she appeared to have a grudge against life; moreover she had a talent for catching other people on a wrong foot. *She* was always right.

Now Miss Euphemia was a gentle soul, who followed submissively in the wake of her dominating elder sister, with patience and meekness, with a gift for pouring oil on troubled waters, calming down not only the servants but – a more difficult matter – Miss Tryphena herself.

The 'girls' – there were four of them, and their ages ranged from the cook, a good fifty, with her 'false front', through housemaid and parlourmaid, each in her late twenties, to the kitchenmaid, a mere nineteen. It took four indoor servants – there were two outdoor men-servants – to look after these two maiden ladies incapable of doing a hand's turn for themselves. This was the Edwardian age.

Actually the girls had a good account to give of themselves. They had got up at the unearthly hour of four o'clock to get forward with the annual spring cleaning of the house – more of a rite than a necessity, since the house was not large – before the ordinary day's work was upon them. This last meant lighting the fires in their mistresses' bedrooms, laying their hip-baths before the fires, carrying up the cans of hot water, and later their sizzling hot good-sized breakfasts: bacon and eggs, toast and home-made butter (their ladies wouldn't hear of shop-butter, neither would the servants), Cornish honey and home-made blackberry jam, with clotted cream. This was the vanished world of before 1914.

There was a silence upon the lamp-lit table heaped with scones and buns, the cups of strong tea steaming. In this unexpected visitation it behoved the cook as senior and having the precedence of position to speak up.

She spoke up reasonably but with firmness. She was the only one in the house who was not afraid of Miss Tryphena — and that included Miss Euphemia; she knew a thing or two about Miss Tryphena that that maiden lady would not care to have uttered. (After all, everyone — even in the best regulated families, as this was — had a skeleton in the cupboard.)

The cook gave her mistress to understand that all was intended for the good of the housework: the girls wanted to get forward with the spring cleaning, washing the paint-work, turning out cupboards, before the day's work proper began and while nobody was up and about.

The implication was that Miss Tryphena had no business being up and about.

She calmed down. 'Well, another time let me know the night before. I wondered what on earth was happening from the noise you were making.'

She drew her nightgown closer around her portly figure and departed to the front hall and up the stairs to another four hours' vigil before she began to stir.

Not that she slept. She was often sleepless.

*

She had much to turn over in the still watches of her nights, which were often aching voids of hopelessness and despair. If anything came up to fill them, it was resentment and reproach, rather than any repentance or remorse. Too active, too masculine a spirit for any of that. That would have been like her sister, if indeed the latter could ever have had anything to repent. The very thought rendered the idea of repentance absurd. It was clear enough that the elder sister, with her experience of life, nourished a contempt for the younger, who had had none.

Yet that experience itself, so long ago now, yet vivid as ever, was the source of her unassuaged bitterness, her unappeasable rage, rather than any humiliation, which ate out her heart, upon which she fed until she was without any human sympathy, her mind turning round and round in her skull. She was a woman turned to stone.

Once a year there came to the house a reminder of that past − though, if it aroused any sympathy in her breast, she did not show it.

Miss Roberts bore an unexpectedly plebeian name for one who was understood to be a kinswoman of this ancient Cornish family of Reskymer. Nor was her appearance in accordance: she was a mousey young woman, dressed in a quiet way though without much taste or discernment. She had the diffident manner of the middle middle-class among whom she had been brought up. Of a passive nullity difficult to describe, if there was one person of the family whom she resembled it was the gentle Euphemia.

Living in London, she came regularly to pass the month of September with the two eldering maiden ladies, when most of the county were away, either in Scotland or abroad, and when even the local gentry were apt to be off on holiday. Miss Roberts's visits were as mousey as her appearance, known to few, she herself to no one.

Only one thing surprised − the extent of her tips: a pound each to the cook and to the maid who looked after her. That was something in those days; the money came from somewhere warm.

But who was she?

Her resemblance to Miss Euphemia put ideas into the heads of the sentimental, feather-brained house- and parlour-maids. But the cook knew. She was not sharing her knowledge with her juniors and subordinates: let them keep on guessing.

Altogether quite a guessing game went on among the three younger girls. But they did not know for sure: one thought one thing, another another; at times one of them would have a different conjecture from what she had had before. Cook kept her secret, and her superiority.

*

A good many years before there had been a good-looking, fox-hunting gentleman of a parson at the church on the hill a couple of miles away from where the Reskymers lived: a fine specimen of muscular Christianity, spoken of with respect by the parishioners and neighbours as Parson Phippen. For some reason, no one knew why, this branch of the Reskymer clan attended his church, instead of that of their own parish, conveniently near in the town, in the suburbs of which they lived. Perhaps there were too many of their clan already ensconced in the front pews of that church for pleasure or convenience; perhaps, since they were of old county stock, they preferred the idea of a country church, small and quiet, to one crowded with townees, stiff with shopkeepers who might have to be recognised by a nod, if not positively spoken to.

So Sunday by Sunday the horses were harnessed to the carriage, and the family was drawn up the steep hill to St Lawrence's, with its tower, unfinished since the Black Death, yet dominating the landscape round. The family consisted then of the parents with their two daughters. Here there was no one to share their unquestioned precedence; the small parish had no resident squire: they occupied the front pew alone. When the Communion cup came to be administered, no-one to march in front, for them to put their lips to the cup *after*.

There being no gentry in his parish, and no one else for company, Parson Phippen was much thrown together with the Reskymers. In young, and vigorous, middle age he was a good many years older than the Reskymer daughters. That would not have been an insurmountable obstacle to his marrying one of them, if only his living had been a somewhat better one. (He was rather good at getting over obstacles anyway.) But though Parson Phippen was indubitably a gentleman of good family — Phippen, it was said, was a corruption of Fitzpen — it was impossible to maintain a family in genteel style on that living;

and the Reskymers expected better matches for their daughters. Rather none at all than that.

So Parson Phippen, full of masculine vigour, more spirits than he knew what to do with or than his fox-hunting could take care of, was thrown back on his bachelordom. A largish country vicarage with a glebe, plenty of room for a family to romp round in, and not a woman to put in it.

However, there was a growing girl with an eye for him. Miss Tryphena, at this stage coltish and already large of limb, with a good seat on a horse − Miss Euphemia was too fearful to go on horseback − used to go out hunting with him. She didn't know what fear was, and would take any fence or ditch alongside of him. Nor had she any fear of a man. Instinct, and his looks, occasionally an arm or hand aiding her, told her what he wanted or needed; she sympathised: she wanted it too.

They became lovers. Love found a way − or, rather, Parson Phippen, agile and observant, found a way.

Miss Reskymer's bedroom, in those days, was at the side of the house − her parents' in front − and it gave on to the orchard. A convenient ladder lay under the shelter of the farther wall; this the muscular clergyman used to manoeuvre on dark nights along the path and get it up against the house to her bedroom window.

It did not take many such nocturnal visits, in those benighted days, before the girl found herself pregnant.

The gardener had noticed the displacement of the ladder, the steps, the marks indicating whose window. But he was not one for making trouble; he knew which side his bread was buttered. He kept quiet. Only it happened that his girl, who was about Miss Tryphena's age, now kitchen-maid in the house, was one day to become cook. Hence how she came to know what she knew.

On the verge of a nervous breakdown, threatened with a 'decline' − though in fact Miss Reskymer had never looked more rosy and buxom − she was sent mysteriously away for a pro-longed cure abroad.

About the time of her expected return, lightened of her burden, a fatal accident to her parents hurried her back. They had been returning from Sunday morning service at St Lawrence when the horses bolted down the steep hill with the hair-pin bend at the bottom, the carriage overturned and the occupants killed.

What were the thoughts of the returning prodigal at the news?

Regret? Remorse? Relief?

Some element of all three were mingled in her emotions, along with passions unallayed, unassuaged, unappeasable.

With the superstition of her race, all the deeper for being instinctive, hardly conscious, she could not help linking the fatal accident to her parents with her own guilt towards them. They had been kind in their fashion, had always meant to do their best, according to their lights, to and for their daughters. She had rewarded them thus.

For, of course, there was a scandal. Though Tryphena's affair was hushed up, and no one knew for certain whither she had gone, or for what purpose, everybody suspected. No one had any doubt about the gist of the matter — still less when Parson Phippen quietly disappeared from the neighbourhood.

But Miss Reskymer was a candid soul, and would not disguise from herself that mingled with the regret, and even remorse, there was relief. She would not now have to face the reproachful eyes of her parents. That ordeal had been removed by an act of God — if God permitted such things. Moreover, to gild the relief, she and her sister emerged co-heiresses to a tidy fortune of £56,000. That was worth something in those days, when gold still circulated from the banks, the pound was worth a pound, the unchallenged master of the world's currencies.

It was more than enough for two maiden ladies to live on for the rest of their lives, even into and after the first world war. For, of course, with such a skeleton in the cupboard, with such a story known at least within the confines of their own class, there was no marriage for either Miss Tryphena or Miss Euphemia.

They lived on, becoming more and more eccentric in their different ways, in their isolation. Few people came to see them; they did not wish to see anyone. In time they ceased to attend the church on the hill. The lawyer-member of the clan, who

attended to their affairs — their well-plushed affairs gave little
trouble — paid his regular visits once a quarter, Michaelmas,
Christmas, Lady day, Midsummer, with changeless, boring
iteration, came round and round.

The younger sister developed the eccentricities that went with
an under-developed will. Used to submitting to her elder sister,
relying upon her in everything, she became incapable of
making up her mind about anything. She became more and
more vague and absent-minded, living her life in a kindly
confusion of her wits.

Her sister exhibited the eccentricities of an over-developed
will. Where the other was absent-minded, she was too present-
minded, always seeking out occasions for complaint, for putting
others in the wrong. Yet she was not ungenerous; with a mania
for tidiness that seemed to bespeak meticulousness about
money, she was in fact open-handed. She was made on a big
scale. Her complaints about wasting her light, and eating her
nice buns, meant nothing in themselves, as the cook well understood. They were just counters in the bitter inner game she
played with herself, cheated by life, cheated of life, herself
capable of giving birth to life, having given birth (once).

So she went round and round in her mind, champing, eating
her heart out, with the irreversible seasons. Would that the
seasons were reversible!

This season, this Michaelmas, Miss Roberts would pay her
discreet and noiseless visit once more, and nobody be any the
wiser.

But before she came this year a period had come to an end in
the history of this unhappy house. With her savage will strained
beyond her reason, Miss Tryphena had determined to put a
period to it all, an end to herself and her misery.

With her instinct for tidiness supporting her crazily to the
last, she carried a pail into the lavatory and neatly cut her throat
into it.

When her will came to be read — generous gifts to all the
servants — and they learned that £30,000, the bulk of her fortune, was left to the annual visitor, Miss Roberts, they no longer
had any doubt that this was indeed her daughter.

XXIII

Captain Pollock's Fields

'Of course they were not his,' said my aunt with some indignation, for she knew the story. 'They belong to Miss Hunkin's family really. Only her father and mother were so easy-goin', and illiterate, that if Mr Pascoe said they were his then they must be his!

'It probably began when Mr Pascoe was at Tretinney farm — takin' those fields over and farmin' them. They were perhaps not of great value then. He paid the Hunkins a small rent — and did them some small service, and the rent was dropped. When the old people died, he said they were his.

'If Mr Pascoe said so — then they must be. The Hunkins were as easy-goin' as that!

'The Pascoes had no children, so they adopted a daughter — Maggie. When Mr Pascoe died he left a will leaving all to Maggie. Of course he intended Auntie Pascoe to have the benefit of it so long as she lived, and *then* to go to Maggie. He never thought that Maggie would die before Auntie did.

'Maggie had married Captain Pollock, captain of a vessel — always away to sea. A swaggerin', blusterin' fellow, with a boomin' voice like Mevagissey fog-horn. When Mr Pascoe died, Captain Pollock took the property and the house in Maggie's name.

'When he came home from sea he *would* take the first place in the house and sit at the head of the table. When Auntie Pascoe was carvin', he'd say:

'"I don't see why I can't do the carvin' in my own house" — and would take the carvin' knife and fork out of Auntie's hands.

'She didn't say anything — only gently:

'"Of course you can, Joe."

'And he couldn't carve for anything – would make some mess of it!

'Well, he made things so unpleasant for Auntie Pascoe that he got her out of her own home. You see, he was thinkin' of marryin' again.

'"All right," she said, "there's a little cottage on the place: I can go in there."

'So she did. She had nothin' else to live on. She had to have parish pay.

'Captain Pollock would sometimes send her money, a cheque, when he was away to sea. He knew he had done wrong. She used to send his money back – post it all back to him.

'"It isn't his," Miss Hunkin would say. "It's ours really."

'However, it didn't do Captain Pollock any good. Maggie died – a nice girl she was. He married again – and his second wife died.

'These last years he was ill – a painful illness, stinkin' like Herod, so that nobody'd want to see him. And he was quite alone – no children by either wife.

'The fields, however, had grown a great deal in value as building sites at Mevagissey – doubled in size since the war.

'"Why don't you see about it, Miss Hunkin?", said my irate aunt. "There must be deeds to the property somewhere."

'"The little money we've got," said Miss Hunkin firmly, "we've had to work hard for. We aren't goin' to throw it away tryin' to get back Captain Pollock's fields."'

XXIV

Dereliction

For all its Cornish name the place was in Devon. I first caught sight of it from an old ridgeway off the main road — the roofs of a large Gothick-looking mansion down in the valley below. What could it be?

I remembered the tombs in the church on the hill back along the road: three armoured esquires shelved on top of each other as in ships' bunks. This was their parish, or not far: those would be the ancestors.

But great was my surprise, when I came to a little church nearer the estate, to find a sophisticated Georgian monument such as one might see in a metropolitan church, not here in the wilds, in the back of beyond.

Reading the inscription I then saw why: the figure of the elegant bust with decorative flourishes was that of a Lord Chamberlain to George II, a name I remembered from the Letters of Horace Walpole. This was at any rate a more recent ancestor than those rebarbative old Elizabethan effigies.

What had happened to the family? And what was the house now?

Time pressed, I had to hurry on, but made a note to come back one day and explore.

It was some time before I was that way again, off the track, and had an opportunity. I went down the unkempt drive, now a mere cart-track, hunks of fallen timber here and there, to confront a house that was a surprise.

It was not Elizabethan after all, nor even 18th century, but early 19th century, Regency Gothic, perhaps by Wyatt or Wyattville, battlemented, turreted, rather grand. Had the family overspent themselves, and thus come to an end? Dereliction was over all.

The house faced east, looking along a flat expanse of turf that had once been a well-kept lawn, dominated by an ancient mulberry tree, a slight corrugation beside it where the ground had been disturbed. Some effort had been made to keep the grass and weeds down, and — yes — there were two rickety garden chairs out in the corner, with a few tools about. The place was at least inhabited, but by whom?

Up to the front door I went, rather queasily, a question mark in mind — to confront a large notice: 'BEWARE OF THE DOG'.

I had no mind to be bitten by a strange dog, so I retreated — frustrated. But not before I had had a glimpse through the glass door, into a large hall filled with a huddle of out-at-heel furniture, piled up like an auctioneer's rooms.

However, no dog appeared, nobody about — utter silence, not even a sound from the bell-turret over the hall. I was at liberty to take in the architecture — did I like it? Not much: it was Regency Gothic on the way to becoming Victorian. Unattractive — and in its present state! — woodwork peeling, launders askew, everything crying out to be put right. What a time one would have, getting it back into condition.

As I went back, past the mulberry tree, up the cart track, I played the familiar game of how I would set about restoring it to its pristine condition. Out of the question — it would cost thousands. All the same, the place would never look right unless kept spick and span — as it was, demeaned, disfigured, disgraced.

*

Before I made my next attempt I did a little research into the history of the old family, who had lived there for centuries, created the place and built the house. And I made some inquiries into the present proprietors.

For, of course, the former family had gone, their possessions dispersed, name lost in female descendants far away in East Anglia. I learned a little about these — how the family silver, what remained of it, had come down to them; some of the furniture had come to another branch of descendants. What of the papers, manuscripts, letters — what interested the historian? No news, no leads.

But I got a lead on the present occupants — a story queer enough in itself. Two bachelors lived there together: one of them of a family at least as old as the ambivalent Carnmarths, ambivalent between Devon and Cornwall through the centuries. The other companion was far from being out of the same drawer — one would have thought servant, or valet: in fact a farmer's son of the locality, who had been in the 1914–18 war with the Captain. They occupied the vast, mouldering mansion — or what of it was livable-in — together: no woman to 'do' for them, no daily; they 'did' for themselves, were sufficient unto themselves.

And I found the clue to their devotion to each other. The Captain, present owner, had been severely wounded on the Western Front and given up for dead. His young devoted batman wouldn't believe it, wouldn't accept it — gave him the kiss of life, remained fixed to his lips again and again, until signs of revival proved him right.

The couple had remained devotedly fixed to each other ever since.

Of course, they were not both wholly received by what remained of county society, to which the Captain by rights belonged. But he did not care to belong to it, itself in some considerable dereliction, like the roof over their heads. '*Pourvu que ça dure*' — as Madame Mère used to say (or rather, in her strong Corsican accent, *Pourvou que ça doure*) — was his attitude: so long as the roof lasts. . . .

But not always did the ceilings last, as I learned without penetrating inside.

I got a line on the house and its inmates from a Cornish cousin of the Captain's, who, as a young man, had actually been allowed to stay a night.

As he went up what had been a grand staircase to his room an owl planed softly, silently over his head and out of the front door. But, *in* his room there was a rumpus in the ceiling in the night, and a large rat plumped through on to his bed.

*

Gathering bits and crumbs of information about this extra-
ordinary ménage — so exciting to the imagination inspired by
the cult of romantic decay — and piecing it together in the
historian's way, I summoned up courage to mount an assault in
proper form. I wrote to the Captain telling him of my interest in
the history of the former family, asking if I might call when next
in the neighbourhood and suggesting a date.

I received a gentlemanly, unexpectedly obliging, reply. He
would be very pleased: *they* would be there on the afternoon of
the suggested date.

Thus fortified, I equipped myself with a friend too, and on
the day we crossed the frontier into Devon, and made for the
Sleeping, or moribund, Princess.

It hadn't occurred to me that we should be frustrated, for
myself the third time defeated. We pulled the cracked bell
beside the front door. No dog appeared: evidently the notice
was just to keep visitors off. No one about. We peered in
through the glass door.

Yes — the front hall was evidently where they lived. A large
sofa, the stuffing out at the corners, in front of a huge fireplace,
though hot summer the heaped ashes of winter or spring fires
not cleared away. Dilapidated armchairs here and there; small
tables piled with out-of-date, untidy periodicals — as it might be
Fields, *Illustrated London News*, *Punches* of former years
undisturbed. In a bookcase a number of tatty books, undescrib-
able. And everywhere old knick-nacks, *bric-à-brac*, bits of
china that might have been good, photographs — more than
ever the interior of a country auctioneer's premises.

What was exceptional was that the walls were covered,
haphazardly, with pictures — like the remains of a family collection. Mostly water-colours, likely enough by some Victorian
maiden aunt, but in the dusky background a few earlier oil
portraits.

And also, what was evident — the place was occupied: this was
their living room; for on a small table here and there were a few
glasses, a whisky bottle, a syphon, the usual accompaniments of
drinking. The dusty, untidy, overladen atmosphere was heavily
masculine. No woman's hand had touched that interior: it

hadn't seen broom or brush or duster for years. A few bits of male equipment lay about: big gum-boots, a haversack, rain-coats, a woollen scarf or two, even the lawnmower was inside. Everything waiting; signs of presence, but no one there — as if the place was under a spell, under an enchantment, bewitched. Was it haunted?

Considerably bewitched ourselves, we prowled round looking in through the windows. We skirted the house to the left, the south side which looked up *against* the slope of the hill. And here we had to scramble up a tumbled little track, the stones peeping through the skeleton of earth, to look into what seemed to be their pantry — or was it their kitchen? The slope upwards made it difficult to see in — a table, more bottles (we supposed they drank a good deal), unwashed plates, débris.

When we got up the bank to the back of the house looking west, we were again frustrated. Evidently the back was one large, tall-windowed ballroom — but shuttered. A crack or two in the shutters didn't give us much of a view: we could see only that it was totally empty, disused, shut up.

We were impressed to silence ourselves, aghast rather, at the spectacle of what had been grandeur fallen upon evil days, everything folding up, falling in, deserted. Why the desertion? What had happened? Moreover, why no one to meet us, when an appointment had been made in due form? Were we being deliberately disappointed, rather laughed at?

*

We *were* disappointed, considerably put out after the effort we had made. We made our way back across the lawn, with the hump under the mulberry tree, and sat waiting for a bit in the garden chairs under the big ilex, mournfullest of trees, sweeping to the ground. Behind us, an overgrown pond, all reeds and weeds. We waited for a bit. Of course nobody turned up.

We crossed the lawn to the cart-track, former drive, which ran — I now noticed — beside what had been the walled kitchen garden. A large enclosure — it would have needed to be large to feed the big household the house maintained in its heyday:

butler, footman, page-boy; housekeeper, housemaids, parlour-maids, kitchen-maids, what not.

Here the brick wall was broken down: one saw that nothing was grown now inside — and what good soil it would have been from centuries of night-soil from such a household! Only one or two scrabbling apple-trees, no fruit; an elder-tree; weeds and brambles and overgrowth up to a man's skull.

There we met a tractor coming down. No Captain or friend — we had given up hope. But we asked the fellow driving where they were.

'Aw, they'm auver to the farm, seein' to the 'arvest.'

'Oh, they have a farm, have they? Is it attached to the place — nearby?'

'Aw, noa. 'Tes a couple o' miles or more away.'

We let the fellow know that we were expected, were not tres-passers: he didn't seem very friendly, perhaps regarded us with the suspicion of a Devonian: we were from over the frontier.

'Are they occupied over there all day?'

'Aw, yes; they'm pretty busy 'bout the 'arvest.'

'What time, then, do they get back?'

'Not till supper-time, not till dusk-like.'

We gave up. We were defeated. Was it deliberate? We rather fancied so, and felt cheated as we made our way out, and looked back over that sad domain.

For all the game we liked to play, for all our fantasying what might be done with it, it was not a promising proposition. The estate occupied a shallow, flat depression in this hilly, semi-moorland country, rather sour land, not good dairy land, though the family must have pastured their cattle here through the ages. Wisps of woodland appeared here and there in the distance — not good timber either, though on the far edge of the estate towards Dartmoor trees were being cut: one heard the whine of a chain-saw. The whole place needed a drastic cam-paign of planting and re-afforestation.

The historic family can never have been rich. Hence their need for office through the centuries. In Elizabethan and Jacobean times they had been Captains of St Michael's Mount in Cornwall, whence they had originated — and hence those armoured effigies in their bunks in the church on the hill. Their original home in Cornwall was well known to be haunted. Was this, to which they had migrated, as well? Was that what had driven them out?

Even in the good Georgian times they had needed office to support their life-style, as we say today. Hence the Lord Chamberlain of the Household to the Hanoverians, and the marriage to a Court lady, something of an heiress. Had that encouraged the splurge into grandeur, and the replacement of a modest Devon manor-house by this white elephant by a Regency Court-architect? Had they overspent themselves, and thus lost their centuries-long hold?

No — it was not even that, but something else. It was the Captain's young cousin with his nose for folk-lore — no relation, any of them, to the original family all dispersed — that told me the macabre story of the place, whether haunted or not, I do not know.

But, in the Victorian age, a strange thing befell there. The family were away abroad one summer, when the page-boy disappeared. This was rather odd and unlike him; the lad had hitherto shown no disposition to wander; he had been attentive to work, rather promising, for he was of an inquisitive West Country turn of mind, apt at looking after (and into) things.

When the family returned, proper inquiries were made for the boy, to no avail. No one had seen or heard of him: it remained a mystery where he had gone.

That autumn there was a shoot, all the beds in the house were full. One of the guests from over the border, a Cornishman, was the least little bit psychic. Before the house went off to bed the subject of the missing page came up, and that night the guest dreamed that the boy had been murdered. Perhaps there was nothing unaccountable in dreaming that — he was of a sort to imagine things; when he told the company his dream, their commonsense pooh-poohed the idea. Things like that didn't happen in the Devon countryside in the reign of dear Queen Victoria.

Nevertheless, the next night he dreamed the dream again. And again on a third night, when he dreamed that, if they dug under the shade of the mulberry tree, the mystery would be solved.

The dream was too insistent, and too circumstantial, to be ignored. The spot was searched, the ground dug, the body found.

It transpired that the boy had been spying on butler and housekeeper, and found them *in flagrante delicto*. The butler had made away with him.

The historian of the family added that the butler was the last man to be hanged at Launceston — a public hanging which people flocked to see from all over the county — before Assizes were transferred to Bodmin. But why the hanging should have taken place at Launceston, instead of Exeter, the historian was unable to say.

XXV

The Ex-Schoolmistress

'She's had a sad life really — Lena,' said my loquacious aunt, coming out from a visit to her, while I had waited an unconscionable time in the car. 'You wouldn't think so really, would you? I mean, to look at her — she's a fine-lookin' woman. But she is sad really.'

They were a large family of brothers and sisters, all clever, but left — call it — not very well cared for. Lena wanted to be a schoolteacher, but didn't get her school certificate.

She then married Jack Dawe, son of the surveyor, since her sister had married his brother. 'Jack Dawe — I never cared much for his looks,' my aunt went on; 'but he was a charmin' man, and Lena was *that* fond of him! . . .

'He went out to Canada for his health, and she went with him. Oh, a long way off — British Columbia, I think, where there were a good many Cornish folk.

'She buried her baby there, and then he died. She picked up and came home right away, bringing their bodies in the ship with her. She said to me, "I felt I couldn't leave them out there and come away. I just couldn't leave them."'

She had them brought home in a large square box — put in together — not like a coffin. She had the grave made ready, and there they are in St Austell cemetery.

She went in to consult Walter John Nicholas. He, a staunch Bible Christian, and Sydney Hassock, as stout a Churchman, were in those days the Box and Cox of our locality, or, rather, of its local government. They shared the chairmanship of the District Council, taking it turn and turn about — I can't tell you how many times each was chairman of that prudent cheeseparing (in those days) body.

Now she had to earn her living: what should she do?

She put the question to Walter John. That worthy pronounced:

'You go and take your School Teaching Certificate.'

So she went away to Exeter, and then she passed her certificate.

*

She had her school out at Gwendra — so called from the white sands of that china clay country. You can see the gleam of quartz in the whitish grey granite of which her little Infants' School was built. There it stands at the end of the hamlet, on the edge of the downs — almost all the menfolk employed in the clayworks in those days.

One day when passing there, my aunt continued, 'I said to Mark, "I should like to look in on Lena" — all the little children were out to play. And Lena said, "You must come and have tea with me in my lodgings."

'I must say she had everything *very* nice.

'Now she is retired and has her own house and pension. And she's married a widower — funny-lookin' man to look at, with big bulgy eyes. But he's a very nice man.

"Not the first time he asked me," said Lena. "I didn't know that I wanted to marry him. But, after all, he's company, and we think the same things, and have the same ideas. And he's a very nice man."

'He's the retired captain of a vessel — Captain Hay.

'You wouldn't think that Lena had that story in her life,' concluded my aunt, 'would you now?'

XXVI

Sandy Trebilcock's Farm

His grandfather was the blacksmith in the village of St Protus and St Hyacinth on the edge of the Moor. All day and every day the merry sound of hammer on anvil would ring out, the big wheezing bellows blow up the glowing fire in the dark interior of the smithy; and there would be the unforgettable smell of scorching horse-hoof at the bottom of the Green, where the horses were shod.

To his busy life as blacksmith and farrier — for all round the edges of the Moor were the farms — old Trebilcock added the occupation of cutler. A lot of people round about had their knives from him (forks were not in much use among them in those days).

Old Trebilcock's wife was a Nancollas of Carslake — thought well of herself as such, though her father was no success as a farmer.

He drank a good deal — just poured the farm down his throat. Such time as he could spare from drinking, he would collect odds and ends of useless information.

He would say to his workmen,

'London wadn' built in a day — what's the 'urry?'

They were in no hurry to set about their work; so they would sit down, and Nancollas would ask:

''Ow many cows' tails would it take to reach to the moon? — Allowin' three feet six inches to a tail?'

He had it worked out. But this bit of information didn't serve to work the farm.

Or down at the pub he would say:

'Me birthday today — drinks on me.'

One day he promised the fellows a jar of gin at his funeral.

'W'en be we to drink et?', they said. 'Before, or after, funeral?'

Nancollas had his answer ready to this:

'Why, *before*. *After*, I shan't be with 'ee.'

He ran through the farm — nothing left when he died — the farm completely run down.

The fool left his youngest child, a girl of six, to be brought up as a parish apprentice.

*

This didn't prevent her from thinking well of herself — she was a Nancollas, after all, of Carslake. When she married Trebilcock, she made him take a farm; she would run the dairy, and take in boarders to help out. And so they did — and made a success of it. She was determined that her son, Sandy, should do better, and sent him to school.

Sandy was very spirited and, as a boy, would occasionally play truant, and ride to hounds on his pony. His father knew this habit of taking a day off from school, when the hounds were out.

Sir Fortescue Warwick was the local bigwig then, and Master of the Hunt. One day Sandy's father looked up from work and saw the Hunt in full cry along the horizon, a boy on a pony at the tail of it.

Trebilcock said to his workman,

'Is that Sandy?'

'Yes, 'tes, maister.'

'Tha's the third time this week 'e's run off after they 'ounds.'

''Tes too bad, 'tes,' said the workman sympathetically.

'An' what damn business is it of yours?' said the proud father.

*

When quite a young man Sandy took a farm of Sir Fortescue. His first year — 1886 — was a year of bad drought, and rebates on farm-rents were made by the landlords. As much as 50 per cent by the Robertses, the most generous of them — as they were among the richest (the tin-mines in the West pouring in their dues then). Some gave a rebate of $22\frac{1}{2}$ per cent.

But his steward refused to give Sandy any rebate at all, on the ground that he had taken his farm for fourteen years at a reduced rent. Sandy did not accept this view: a drought was a drought, something exceptional — and applied to all.

At the Court dinner held at Michaelmas there were compliments and thanks proposed to Sir Fortescue for his generosity — his $12\frac{1}{2}$ per cent generosity.

When the lord of the manor rose to speak, he graciously recognised the good spirit of the tenants; his family had long known that they could be relied on to understand *his* difficulties, as *he* (drawing himself up grandly) understood theirs, etc., etc. But — there was one young fellow who had not exemplified good spirit — though in fact he already had his farm at a reduced rent.

At this all the cock in Trebilcock's name rose to his head, and he flatly contradicted the great man. When Sir Fortescue argued that the reduction of rent covered the contingent loss from drought, Sandy, without rising, added, for good measure:

'That's a lie!'

The lord of the manor had never before been so spoken to in his own parish — regularly bearded, and by a youngster too. It was a tense moment, and great excitement among the farmers — and waiters all agog — in the big court-room of the 'Britannia'. Nothing had been known like it before.

Taken aback, and flustered, Sir Fortescue paused in his tracks. He took time to think — not a frequent or easy operation with him. He saw Sandy as a boy on a farm pony at the tail-end of the Four Burrow. At last he came up with a thought — a fence the young man wouldn't be able to take:

'Well, one may do what one likes with one's own property — would you, young man, like to give up your lease?'

'Is that a promise?' said Sandy stoutly; and added, 'It's no threat to me.'

'Yes,' said Sir Fortescue. 'I'll see to it that no landlords in the county have a farm available for so ungrateful and ill-mannered a young cub.'

No more following the hunt for young Sandy.

*

This event was about the time of Lord Randolph Churchill's

celebrated remark that he had 'forgotten Goschen'. Likewise Sir Fortescue Warwick had forgotten a newcomer to the ranks of landlords in the county — a newcomer whom he had snubbed.

The new man belonged to the remarkable family of Willament, who had played such a part in the industrial development of the county, in tin and copper mining, smelting, laying tracks for transport; founding a bank to finance these operations; running the stores that supplied the mines, and the truck-shops at which the miners had to deal. At every stage, with every link in the chain, this redoubtable family made a profit. Their fortune was immense.

For a generation now the Willaments had been moving into land, picking up an estate here and there from a tired or improvident old family, and applying the initiative and business acumen which had built up their fortune to the downward dive that had overtaken agriculture with the arrival of cheap American corn from the late 1870's. British industry, which built the railways to the Middle West, had dealt a blow at the old landed interest.

With Sir Fortescue Warwick it was no such consideration but simple, antiquated snobbery that led him to question the admission of the Willaments to the County Hunt Ball — that shibboleth by which the old county families kept the edge over new wealth, however great. Sir Fortescue had been defeated; the newcomers were 'in' — to receive a distinctly cold greeting from the Master of the Four Burrow.

This had not been forgotten by the Willament family, whose head had purchased a positively ducal estate spanning the Tamar.

The alert mind of the elder Willament recognised a promising young farmer of spirit when he heard of one — *his* steward was his talent-scout. Sandy was immediately offered a good, if small, farm on the formerly ducal estate.

His last months on Sir Fortescue's premises were lucky — he unexpectedly had flush crops — and sold them standing at a good price. He was able to shake Sir Fortescue's dust off his feet

— which he did with a vengeance — enter on his new farm ready to sow his own crops and with *capital*.

*

The Willament steward made an early call on Sandy to see how he was doing on his new farm.

Was he satisfied with the farm?

'All in good order,' said Sandy.

'Buildings to your liking?'

'Yes. No fault to find.'

'Nothing needed?'

Not that Sandy could see.

The two went indoors, the steward to ask Sandy's wife if she were content with her new home.

'Is there anything we can do for you?'

'Well,' said Mrs Trebilcock, 'I *have* been used to a garden. Here, there are only two tiny plots in front of the house. But at the back there is a small, disused quarry that would make a good garden.'

Out of this quarry the stone to build the farm and farm-buildings had been scooped, in time past.

'What an excellent idea! — never thought of it,' said the steward.

— 'If fenced off from the cattle,' said Sandy's wife, timorously, afraid of asking too much — and envisaging a wooden fence.

Next week down came the builders from the big house, who built a stone wall across the entrance to the quarry to keep out cattle, and put up a proper gate. The week after, a couple of gardeners arrived — the Willaments were already making a new name as gardeners. They laid out the garden, carted down manure, planted fruit trees and berries — built up the soil, all in good time.

Sandy and his wife were well content there, and did so well that — after the first term of their lease was out — they graduated to a larger farm.

A still bigger and more important one was offered them in West Cornwall, where the Willaments were strongly entrenched

— their original stamping-ground (and indeed they owned most of the mine-stamps operating there).

But Sandy was an East Cornishman — and no proper East Cornishman would wish to up stumps for West Cornwall, any more than a Cornishman from the West would feel at home in East Cornwall.